Chapter 1

The Unexpected Deliciousness of Mail

It is of course, a matter no longer open to discussion. Amongst the principal parties concerned, the subject is one that is most decidedly, almost definitely, sort of, closed, for as Kitty is fond of saying: "Since we were all here, we were all there when it happened."

So, unless the old human female, Victoria, has lost her senses, again (as history strongly suggests as possibility), and is completely mistaken, she is certain that no one of them wishes ever again to be reminded of that sad event. It is with the greatest reluctance then, that this narrator has been forced by necessity to exhume the old story in all its gory details, since we are well aware that once told, it cannot be untold. Once heard, it cannot be unheard.

Indeed Miss Kitty has smugly taken to admonishing the old woman, "One cannot, for all the pandas in China, put the elephant back in his bottle."

Wildlife. Nature, raw in tooth and claw. The one word encapsulating it best is: Gardening. Though sparse, errant blades of vigorous weed-variety grasses would protrude wildly seeded heads around fence posts and at the base of stone walls, and more pointedly to the development of this narrative, up through the cracks in the otherwise well-regulated grey concrete sidewalk slabs marching in stodgy parallel parade past the fenced-in private garden at the public front of the house. This display was especially vibrant at the base of the mailbox post at the curb. Officious city employees took notice, and soon threatening calls to action were littering the polished surface of Victoria's immaculate kitchen table.

Two friends, the human, Victoria and the four inch tall plastic toy bear, Miss Kitty, were dismally sorting through the pile of letters, each in differing attitudes. Victoria was slumped in her hard chair, elbows splayed on the mirror-smooth, vast table top. Her aching grey-haired head reposed wearily between her arthritic hands. Drips caused by seasonal allergies fell from her swollen red nose, which she caught up more often than not in a lace-edged hankie.

"Whatever am I to do now?" she pondered aloud. "I certainly do not have the strength to run that heavy gas weed-whacker, at least not now, or the flexibility to squat down cross-legged like a yogi on the sidewalk in order to pull out all those clots of razor-sharp grass. I certainly do not have the inclination nor the bankroll to ferret out a cheap reliable gardener, for as far as I know, they are mythical creatures. Like winged unicorns and cheap reliable plumbers. Fairyland beings who no longer exist. Where does one go from here?"

In contrast to the limp flesh of the ridiculously drooping human, Miss Kitty was a staunchly impervious, rigidly unchangeable, plastic ball of energy, imperiously stomping around, sometimes skidding perilously close to the edge of the polished tabletop, as she made it her business to flip the unopened yet obviously ominous envelopes with a hind paw. Suspiciously, she stooped to take a gourmet's sniff.

"Hmm." An intriguing notion, to be sure. "Unless I am mistaken," she muttered to herself, "and I seldom am, here be a garlic lover." She sniffed again, and then licked one especially appealing envelope. "Yes!" Her epicurean nose twitched with greed and delight. "Oh, yes!" she chortled with surprised approval. She became lost.

Victoria was recalled from her melodramatic navel gazing by the startling notice of Kitty's employment. "Please, do stop licking my mail!" She bent her head closer. "Are you...?" She adjusted her bifocals. "Tell me you are not chewing my mail!"

Kitty raised happy, glittering eyes to her friend's incredulously twisted face. "Ham, Victoria! Ham and Swiss cheese. Upon the envelopes. After having passed through so many hands; hands intimately involved in conveying foods to mouths. Snacks. You, who have not the keen senses of a bear, do not know. You do not know. You cannot know."

A long suffering witness to Kitty's appetites as well as a sometimes reluctant partner in her unquenchable curiosity as well as a firm tamper for her irrepressible animal responses,

Victoria merely sighed. "I suppose that's true." Other concerns oppressed the elderly human.

She stared unseeing out the kitchen window where soft summer greenery, tiny, indistinguishable leaves of a vast assortment fluffed about on invisible soft warm breezes. Sunlight flickered, dappling the window like the patting of the little paws of a cat or squirrel or vole. Pat pat pat. Another sound much nearer, from inside the room recaptured her attention, directing it back to the table top, now quite littered with damp shreds of chewed up paper. The toy bear masticated wetly; eyes closed.

"Kitty! My dear! If you are feeling so peckish at this particular hour, we still have part of a melon, and some cheese in the refrigerator. You need not eat paper." Automatically, the woman hoisted herself from her seat, preparing to fetch the more conventional foodstuff for her impetuous friend. She was halted by a blissful sigh.

"Do not trouble yourself, dear Victoria. I am quite content. Sated to repletion."

Indeed, judging by the mounds of damp paper heaped up all around her, Kitty had partaken of a substantial meal indeed. Snowdrifts of paper, sandbars, dunes, lay in abundance across the table top.

"I do hope there are no ill-effects from your unusual repast," observed the old woman politely. "Not very nutritious,

I'm afraid, and a little heavy on the fiber." Not usually prone to sarcasm, Victoria's recent bad news had rendered her a trifle touchy.

"Well, you should know." was Kitty's inarticulate response. The bear was afloat on post-feast contentment.

This reference to Victoria's doctor-ordered, viciously-resented, gleefully-ignored, healthy new diet was a low swipe. Irritation bubbled up.

Victoria suddenly realized just how very large had been Kitty's feast, when she could not find an intact shred of any one of the letters. "Kitty! This is beyond anything! There were phone numbers, and important times scheduled on those papers. Now you've eaten them all up! How am I supposed to know what I am to do?"

Thirsty after her meal, the bear avidly licked tepid drops of sugary tea from Victoria's saucer. Her attention fully engaged by this newest delightful occupation, she waggled a paw in the woman's direction, dismissing all humans and their ridiculous concerns. "You must do what you must do, when you are required to do it, of course. You, of all people, should know that."

Delightful Tastes

One should be careful indeed not to allow oneself to become seduced by the random encounters with every wafting aroma. But for all practical purposes, the faintest of scents on ordinary envelopes must reveal to the sensitive-snouted the unmistakable evidence of a postal worker's luncheon. Here are delights indeed! Ham and Swiss cheese; a garlicky bologna; peanut butter and honey. Such midday feasts are practically begging the quick-tongued to indulge.

Chapter 2

The Sadness of Entropy

Victoria was mumbling to herself. "I guess I'll just have to get out there on my knees after all, especially now that I have no idea whatsoever of the time frame. I'll just have to try and cut down or root out all that grass. What in the world am I to do with the dandelions? They've always gotten the better of me in the past. That's when I was a good deal more fit than I am now to deal with them. Monsters!"

Every gardener should feel free to commiserate with the sentiment; for dandelions are monstrous things indeed! Victoria continued on with her mumbling, a habit well evolved over the years, years spent sharing her thoughts exclusively with a four inch tall and generally unsympathetic listener. "I wonder, where have all my tools got to? Are they in the garden shed? Surely, they must have rusted after all this time." Another worry to contend with. She shook her head, causing the old gray tendrils of hair to dance.

In preparation for vigorous and unaccustomed outdoor exercise, she rooted around in the cupboard under the stairs hopefully looking for tools and found there instead the sadly dust-covered food and water bowls belonging to the long deceased Alice, the black dog. These relics had been kept as a kind of memorial to that astonishing canine. Alice's owner sighed deeply, but as usual her sighs were for herself alone. Further investigation uncovered some objects of interest. She shook out and donned a pair of stout canvas pants, the knees much stained and rubbed, a thick flannel shirt, wool socks, cracked rough-soled gardening shoes, and lastly, a floppy-brimmed straw hat bedecked with a few moldering paper roses.

She chuckled at the hat. "I do hope Kitty will not notice that this is the hat I used to wear to all those tea parties! Years and years of tea parties!" The hat creased fore and aft, making a kind of dusty cave for the old woman's face. "I shall not be able to see or feel any sunlight, if indeed, I am able to see anything at all." Thus armed against the menace of assault from the outdoor elements, though sneezing ferociously from the assault of the elements indoors, she groped her way, still chuckling, outside to the garden shed.

That rustic small building was showing its age. Cracks in the wood allowed shafts of light to migrate from the backside clear through to the front where they played mischievously about her feet. "No, I haven't really been maintaining things as I ought. Ooh!" Her tentative grasp on the wooden door knob caused one ghastly, ear-splitting creak to issue from the hinges before the pins sheared apart and split in half, causing the door to drop down almost upon her toes. "Oh dear!"

This shed had in the past been the scene of one of Victoria and Kitty's most fractious disputes. The ARA, or Animal Rights

Association, the militant arm of that allegiance of wild animals residing in Victoria's backyard, and dependent upon her for their constant supply of nuts, seeds, and suet, had found in the small plastic bosom of Miss Kitty a most willing and indignant ally. Their grievances were many.

When brought to the human's attention in a particularly pompous and unpleasant way by their "sworn representative", Victoria had been forced under duress into relinquishing her happily innocent role of bird-watching nature-lover and was made to assume the more strenuous and less pleasant role of supply wagon. Indeed, a large red metal wagon with white wings painted on the sides was the only option available for the transporting of the fifty pound bags of feed the ARA demanded. The garden shed had been commandeered, the seed distributed upon shelves inside, and the animals left to their own appetites and devices, all without any more human intervention than what was required and permitted as per the too-frequent notice given by Kitty when supplies were become dangerously low.

When even that task proved too much of a burden for her tired worn-out body, Victoria had quietly relinquished it. This she did without first notifying the ARA's sworn representative, as oath-bound to do those many years ago. Instead, she simply reverted to filling the ordinary wooden feeder (nailed atop a convenient, centrally located post) with cupfuls of seeds scooped from the modest bag kept on the floor inside the kitchen door rather than attempting to wrestle with the expected and taken-for-granted bucketsful. Dutiful as ever, she dared the ARA members to complain, and indeed, was not surprised when there were no complaints, either officially from the sworn representative, or from the many-times-removed generations of ARA descendants. Secretly, the woman suspected the ARA of having naturally disbanded when the last of its members died off. Wild animals after all, have a much briefer lifespan out of doors compared to plastic toys or even pampered humans sheltering inside snug houses.

White chocolate mice.

Heat pieces of white chocolate and cups of cream till melted. Pour into mouse-shaped molds. Allow to set, then unmold and eat as many as possible before Victoria gets to them.

Chapter 3

The Unexplored Deliciousness of Books

Victoria shakily propped the splintered shards of the shed door to one side and stepped cautiously into the damp and gloomy interior. It was musty, with the organic stench caused by the decaying of all that detritus; those years of seeds and animal droppings and Lord knows what else. Victoria waited some moments for her eyes to adjust before further entering the dark space. "Caution is the mother of...if I want to avoid putting myself at risk from a misstep."

"Whew! What an odor!" This from the intrepid Miss Kitty, who had recovered from her meal and come all unnoticed, determined to plunge energetically past the toe of Victoria's shoe.

The human unceremoniously plucked up her friend between thumb and forefinger. "You will not want to venture onto the floor of this shed, at your height; that I can assure you! If you were taller–but that is beside the point. At this moment, at your height, you should quite sink in over your head and be swallowed up in all that nasty muck."

For once, Kitty was silenced. Indeed, the gloomy atmosphere demanded a good deal more bravery than even she was capable of mustering. "Foolishness," the bear declared at last, though in a tinny voice. She allowed herself to be settled onto Victoria's shoulder, where by clutching her friend's ear and collar, even a very small child's toy might feel safely ideally situated for long-distance viewing. "One niggling little observation. my dear. I feel I must just comment upon it again, as I have in the past. The extraordinary distance existing between yourself and the rest of the world due to your gigantically inconvenient size places you at considerable disadvantage, for how can the mountain understand the squirrel when the mountain does not know the squirrel exists?"

The human came to an abrupt halt. She snatched the bear from her shoulder and, in the dim light and adjusting the distance for bifocals, brought Kitty close to her face. "Why, may I ask, have you begun speaking in this curious manner? Bringing up these odd maxims. I meant to ask before. Have you been reading again? Confucius perhaps?" If the question ended on a somewhat apprehensive note, it was due entirely to Victoria's past experiences with the toy bear.

The bear hemmed and hawed and looked askance, for she had indeed been on another of her periodic rampages through the books in the human's library, with mixed results. She stroked the human's forefinger with a blunt claw. "Too many novel ideas, too much attempting at original thought, my dear. Quite a cacophony! A multitude of innovative stabs at five minutes of fame and glory. I will henceforth control my tongue."

"Your tongue is not the problem, as you very well know, unless...you have not been licking my books as well? Pray, tell me you have not been licking my books!"

Kitty's silence spoke volumes.

"I say, you really must make haste to assure me at once that you have not been licking the pages and bindings of my treasured books, or I shall be quite angry indeed!"

The claw dug a little deeper into the finger. "Allow me at once to give you the assurance you crave, hasty one! I am innocent of such barbarous behavior, especially since I am all too aware of how highly you value your possessions. By the way..." The bear tilted back her head, squinting her eyes, making a narrow observation of the object on Victoria's head. "That hat– that isn't...?"

"Then I am relieved, since you say that you have not been at the books!" The touchy subject of her hat averted, Victoria returned the bear to her shoulder as she returned to her theme; however, within herself, she vowed to examine the individual tomes, searching for evidence of saliva and crumbs, "for that would be death to a book. But, just one moment. Have you re-shelved the books?" It was exceedingly uncomfortable, twisting her head around to talk to the bear clutching her ear, however the alternative was to endure that maddening clawing of her hand. "All helter-skelter, or where they belong? The last time it took me forever to pull them all out from under the couch and behind the cushions, and who knows where all they were stashed. I found one under the refrigerator! If only you would practice tidiness as a general rule of conduct, we should not continue to have to address this issue. Ouch!" There had come an entirely inadvertent tightening of the claws on the human's earlobe.

"So sorry! But, once again, dear friend, I am guiltless of such folly."

However, once again, Victoria privately vowed caution when sitting down upon the over-stuffed living room furniture when next she was so inclined, that she might not inadvertently gouge her back upon a sharp corner of one of the mislaid volumes. Such a thing had happened before, with an evilly-positioned encyclopedia "Experience, as you know…"

That thought unfinished, the subject dealt with, the human hoped her friend was cautioned on the need for extraordinary consideration due to a recent occurrence. Victoria, you may remember, had suffered a stroke. The peculiar turn of her mental deficit had led her, while in a coma, to become Kitty-sized, to wander in Kitty's world, over the past Christmas. This episode was of course one quite forgot by the bear, who found such memory lapses convenient.

That most troublesome thing, a philosophical argument without resolution, was at the root of it all. The human was large, the bear small. The human was a living biological being, the bear a factory-made plastic toy. The human had aged, the bear was unchanged, remaining exactly as she had been for all these many years. The human had always been the one forced to make adjustments and concessions and adapt herself to differing circumstances. The bear had not.

Honestly, though reluctantly, Victoria considered herself the better for it. For instance, she had been prodded by Kitty into practicing an extraordinary degree of microscopic sensitivity to the plight of the very small. Her unusual willingness to enter into the feelings of wild creatures was unheard of amongst her disdainful fellow humans. Her fellow human members of the Garden Club, of which she had been an outstanding participant, were aghast. Victoria suspected them of laughing at her behind her back, but since she was no longer subjecting herself to the whims of the members of that circle she no longer knew or cared what they thought.

The stroke, as devastating as it was, and the unintentional size reduction, had been educational. Victoria could hardly hope to achieve more than she had at the bear's instigation, for selfishly, she would not suffer another cerebral incident just to please her. She was what she was for the time being and refused to apologize for it. However, Kitty might benefit from the occasional reminder that any sudden mental shocks or unexpected physical exertions were to be avoided, lest a repetition might ensue.

Brawnshwieger Sausage

Don't know, don't care. Besides bacon, the best thing ever. EVER! And kielbasa.

Chapter 4

Spider and Other Unpleasantness

The woman gingerly tiptoed onto the floor of the garden shed, trying her best to ignore the moistly squishing muck encasing her shoes, snatching up hand tools as she went. "I have no intention of making this trip twice," she assured Kitty. A three-pronged weeder, hand pick, clippers, trowel, a disgustingly slimy pair of leather gloves, a small shovel, and the errant rake, were awkwardly cradled in her arms or shoved into pockets. She was bent forward, examining the promising contents of a dark corner when her forehead met with a strange resistance. She suddenly jerked back as recognition set in, her head entwined in a very large cobweb. "ULLP!" she gasped and backpedaled as fast as she was capable of moving, swatting at the sticky web and pulling it out of her hair. "OOUGH!" At the moment she burst backwards out of the shed into the hot sunshine, shuddering with disgust from head to toe, she realized Kitty was no longer atop her shoulder.

"Kitty? Kitty, where are you?" she called. Understandably, the woman could not immediately attend to the dire fate that might even now be assailing her friend until the tough strands of webbing containing the desiccated corpses of innumerable insect were frantically brushed from her clothes and hair. A throbbing at her temples, a faintness in her chest, preoccupied her and so some time passed till she felt master enough to resume the retrieval of her friend. "Kitty!" she called weakly, "I say, are you all right?"

A muffled something or other, an outraged growling, a violent verbal explosion, issued forth from within the dank darkness of the shed. Victoria peered helplessly, bracing herself against the doorway while her eyes adjusted. She was made aware of an incongruous sight. There was a wildly flailing object suspended midair from the ceiling, swinging like a pendulum to-and-fro. Muttered threats caused the human's ears to redden.

There was a sudden spasm of movement. With an eruption of language, something went sailing through the doorway to land in the grass at Victoria's feet. The woman stooped anxiously beside her distraught friend, but wisely kept helpful fingers firmly out of harm's way. Help was clearly needed, and readily available, and only too anxious to be delivered, but one has learned in such cases that unless one is indifferent to pain and blood, slashing claws and gnashing teeth, raised voices and heightened emotions, help must wait till it is requested.

As expected, a bedraggled, tightly wound Miss Kitty, slashed at her silken cocoon with sharp claws and dangerously snapping teeth, and was soon freed of the majority of the snare. "Victoria," Kitty uttered in a tremulous voice, "I am in some difficulty. I find I need…will you be so good as to assist me please?"

Victoria proved herself only too willing to oblige, quickly and efficiently removing the last tatters of web the bear had been unable to reach. Thoroughly brushed and cleaned, the toy stood trembling, a four inch tower of outrage. "I never! I shall…well, I shall…I once actually hosted that particular spider, or perhaps her nearest kin, at a tea party under the pine tree. You may remember that incident. Though she skulked inside a funnel-shaped web for the entire time refusing to come out, or perhaps not; whatever the case, I shall never, ever…after being subjected to such barbarity! Suck the life blood from me, will you? I sincerely hope she injured herself or broke off a fang trying to pierce my plastic hide!"

Victoria was startled. "Kitty, my dear! The spider actually tried to bite you?"

"Not only tried, nearly succeeded! After wrapping me so tightly I was incapable of movement, she descended upon me with such a look of cold malevolence! I was helpless to stop the attack. When she had seized me in her jaws, I felt quite faint, I can assure you, but upon feeling her close with the back of my neck I recovered the use of my limbs as well as my voice! That was one startled spider, I can assure you, Victoria! Now, let us proceed. I intend to make good on my threats to burn the place down. I am quite myself again. I shall just hurry into the house and fetch the matches. Are they still in the cupboard by the sink?"

Things Warmed Over

Sometimes things that have been kept refrigerated for whatever mysterious human purposes for a length of time are found to have lost all taste and odor due to the cold temperatures. Invariably, most things taste much better warmed up a little. Not cooked, mind you, just warmed. Everyone knows there is no sense in saving food for later or a rainy day. What happens if it doesn't rain?

Chapter 5

Nonexistent Neighbors

Much later, the frustrated arsonist and her human confounder bleakly surveyed the tall grass spikes from the street opposite the front sidewalk. The bear still convulsively bristled at the memory of her recent traumatic encounter in the garden shed, causing her fur to stand quite on end and making her look, so Victoria thought privately, like a stubby brownish bottlebrush. All sincere sympathy, the woman refrained from mentioning the uncanny resemblance while steadfastly changing the subject.

One of Kitty's most endearing attributes was her facility for being easily distracted, and as her mind was one naturally attracted to calmness and tranquility, she had taken deep breaths, consciously relaxing her rigid plastic limbs, and allowing her focus to be redirected from revenge and fire to the human's interests and only reverting once every minute or so back to her own inflammatory grievances with a spasm and a growl.

"Well, Kitty, there is nothing to be done about it. Once I drop these stiff old bones down on the sidewalk, I can assure you I shall not be shoveling them back up again any time soon. Probably not for some time, so you must be prepared to be patient. Lunch will most likely be delayed. Perhaps even tea. I am prepared to venture that even supper may have to be forgotten. I may be too tired to cook."

The toy bear's eyes glittered. Victoria allowed a smirk to crease her lips in a private amusement. Kitty did so love her regular meals. However, upon closer examination, Miss Kitty sparkling ocular orbs might have revealed not so much greed, an emotion expected of a bear of such well-scheduled appetites, as it did glee.

The phenomenon went un-remarked by her human friend, who was busy efficiently assembling her tools around her within easy reach. There was a thermos of hot sugary tea standing attention beside the thickly folded blanket, this last article having been deemed necessary for cushioning the hard concrete of the sidewalk. Hanging onto the mailbox post for dear life, the woman flopped down into a sort of inadvertent lotus position, whereupon she began tearing and clipping and digging and pulling away for all she was worth at the knee-high green things obstructing the sovereign right of passage of a righteous public over the thoroughfare.

The work was less challenging than she'd imagined, for as it happens so often, the anticipation of problems had produced overwhelming worries which resulted in a paralysis of action. The work itself was in reality just one of those things best got through by sitting down to it and taking one step at a time. One weed, one handful, in meticulous order, omitting not even the smallest blade of grass, this program soon led to a cleared area the respectable size of which lent to Victoria's sweat-dripping character-wizened face an expression of justifiable pride.

No human feet passed by, conveying grouchy neighbors about their legitimate business. There was no one but Kitty with whom she might share her triumph. She sank back and allowed the aching muscles in her shoulders to relax. That lack of passers-by cast a discordant note over the proceedings. "If my weeds are such a cause for official consternation, then where are the complainants? You know, Kitty, I believe there has not been a single human by here at all the whole of this morning!"

Indeed, Victoria's house did stand in splendid isolation at the end of the street in a kind of cul-de-sac, and it is true that few visitors ever had reason to amble by that way. The woman had become increasingly oblivious to this fact since her sadly curtailed life was now primarily contained within the house proper as well as its magnificent walled garden.

Victoria, you see, had deteriorated. Age will do that to a person, even one as robust as this human had been. The afore-mentioned primary manifestation of her disintegration; the unfortunate lapse in mental state precipitated by an equal lapse in her physical health, had been startling to say the least. That a normally sized human being should have been reduced, like Alice in Wonderland, down to a tiny bit of a speck, a tad shorter than her dear friend Miss Katherine A. Bear, was not a thing at which to sneeze. That wholly unanticipated predicament, and her dramatic reinstatement shortly afterwards to full size, full competency, and a full life, were still a source to her of both pleasure and pain.

Now that she was considered by the experts of medical science to be recovered, the doctors had released her back to her own home, with conditions. The restraints made upon her freedom of movement, the amount of pills she was expected to digest, the dietary affronts to her palate; all these things, while guaranteeing a long life, could not recommend to her one worth living. Taking the matter into her own hands as well she should, she threw out the pills, ate as she was accustomed to eating, and thumbed her nose at the well-meaning but infinitely irritating and intrusive attendants who would call on the phone leaving vaguely threatening messages on the answering machine and even besieging the house sticking further vaguely threatening messages in the screen door.

And where, might you be wondering, is Lily? Victoria's daughter and Kitty's incomparable Butler, having grown up and moved away to her own home, had moved on once again, to another continent, with a husband and a new baby. These engrossing objects in her life eliminated any possibility that she should be available to check up on her mother or enforce the conditions she had been so responsible for putting into place.

When she called on the phone, as she did every week, Victoria made a heroic effort to sound cheerful, and mentally stable.

It is only fair to observe that had Lily known of her mother's ruse, or been aware of the balking at doctors' orders, she must have been on top of things in a moment. Her character was ever one of decided temperament and swift action. So, the yard work, which Victoria fiercely (but falsely) claimed for herself as the best therapy possible, was an oversight. Lily could not have realized how unfit her mother now was to perform such formidable tasks, though she believed she did a fine job taking care of the ordinary household things otherwise.

There was one area in which the daughter had been in firm agreement with her mother; the Butler absolutely resisted any attempt by the medical professionals to separate Victoria from Kitty. Medical strangers, should not be expected, even with the best intentions, to understand the enduring strength and depth of a lengthy relationship between an adult human woman and her adult child's tiny toy bear, and so their well-intended advice was abandoned without a qualm. Victoria and Kitty, it was, against the world, taking no prisoners, and giving no quarter.

Jelly

OH! OH! Dare I say it? Sometimes better than honey!
Especially the lumpy kind.

Chapter 6
The Mailman Cometh

Victoria's treacherous wristwatch indicated she had been working for a little more than two hours, though the excruciating pains gripping her back and hands and knees and shoulders and shins convinced her the time spent pulling weeds was at least twice that.

"You never know about Time!" she murmured, quoting Miss Kitty. "Well, no one will be able to complain now!" She looked around with triumph while struggling gracelessly from her numb knees to her numbed feet. The tallest blade of grass trimmed with the clippers was only half an inch high. The sturdiest weeds had been dug up, roots and all, and were heaped neatly atop a piece of newspaper waiting to be rolled up and left on the curb for garbage collection. The scrupulous woman had even stripped all the moss and tiny wildflowers from out of the cracks between the sidewalk slabs. These innocent and beneficial plants awaited replanting within the boundaries of the fenced-in front garden, for "Then only you and I shall ever see these living jewels, Kitty, and therefore only you and I shall be able to enjoy them or be inconvenienced by them. Those busybodies from the medical clinic who insist on invading my privacy, coming inside the fence, through the garden all the way up to my door, will just have to goose-step a little higher to get over them."

With that happy thought in mind helping to overcome the pain of the kink in her back, she hunched like Quasimodo, using the rake to tidy up the small amount of disarranged greenery. Hurrying now, she retreated from the public sidewalk through the gate to safety behind her own fence. Victoria had to acknowledge that she was becoming downright uncomfortable outside the fence and looked to her barricaded, snug, and some might say, fantastical, life as an oasis. With surprising quickness she crab-walked up the three steps, crossed the entryway, and was safely back inside the cool sanctuary of her home. The door clicked shut behind. She drew in a deep breath. The relief was short-lived. The silence was too silent. She turned her head with difficulty to examine the unaccountable emptiness on the top of her shoulder. She was quite alone.

"Kitty? Kitty, my dear! Oh! Where on earth are you got to now?" Somehow the bear had been forgotten somewhere outside. At once, feeling quite ashamed, she flung open the door and made her way back out to the front garden, from whence she had just fled. She pushed through the gate to the sidewalk, the scene of so much recent industrious activity. "Now, Kitty, how could I have forgotten you?" No small toy bear was to be seen. "Where did I last...?"

True, she distinctly remembered speaking to the bear, as usual. But now she was unable to recall exactly where it was the bear had been, or what had been her answers. Indeed, a review of the past hour left her quite uncertain if the bear had been with her at all. Still, the effort at retrieval must be made without delay as Kitty must have fallen asleep, or found an intriguing flower to sniff, or a hapless insect to eat. The woman searched high and low, and even undid the newspaper bundles of weeds, all in a vain effort to uncover her tiny friend's whereabouts.

It would never do for a grown woman, even one not besieged by teeming swarms of non-existent irritable passers-by, to be heard screeching frantically, calling for a toy bear. So unrefined! Victoria had learned her lesson. The stint in the hospital under medical supervision had given her a healthy allergy to any further impertinent interference. "After all, it is my own life," she had declaimed back then, "and I am certainly capable of making my own decisions, especially about with whom I wish to share it."

This militant attitude regarding the continuation of an innocent friendship of many years' duration with a plastic toy, against the sternest doctors' advice, would, if known, have surely landed her in a private suite at a sanitarium for the mentally unstable. The high fences, latched gate, and firmly locked doors of her home protected much more than just her privacy.

"Kitty," she coaxed in a stage whisper, "Miss Kitty, please, dear friend, do answer me at once!" The tour of discovery, with the human nonchalantly strolling along, although in a somewhat crabbed and lurching fashion, about her front gate, pleading in loud whispers from the side of her mouth for the urgent response of her toy bear, became ludicrously drawn out. "What on earth am I doing?" she demanded. "I know firsthand how stubborn that pestilential animal can be, and how single-minded. She must…"

To her extreme embarrassment, one of those non-existent passersby had materialized, and was at her elbow, gazing inquiringly into her face. Victoria laughed nervously and leaned for support upon a fence post. "Heh, heh, heh," she managed weakly. It was the mailman. Indeed, the same mailman who was most likely the author of the original officious disturbance of her privacy, now had the effrontery to disturb her again.

This unimpressive person said nothing, merely nodding, a slight but precise incline of the head accompanied by a lowering of the eyes, politely formal, yet casual, as if the spectacle of old women chatting aloud to themselves were one of the many everyday occurrences a mailman was expected to endure. His silent greeting acknowledged, he turned a shoulder, and opened the mailbox door, preparing to complete the circuit of his appointed rounds by shoving the advertising circular inside, though the person to whom it was addressed, "Current Occupant," was plainly currently occupying the space right there in front of him.

With one hand still on the latch, and the other outstretched towards the box to relieve it of its load, he paused. He slammed the mailbox door shut. He took one deliberate step back, pivoting to face her. Making eye contact, the man remarked in a low, tremulous voice, "Madam, I believe that for which you are seeking is here," He indicated the mailbox with a nod of his head, and without further comment, brushed past her without relinquishing her mail.

Victoria turned in puzzlement to watch him stalking rigidly away and saw quite distinctly that he balled up the circular and tossed it with a disdainful gesture into the gutter. "How very odd! What an unpleasant person." She addressed the mailbox. "Kitty? Kitty my dear, how could you possibly...why are you hiding in there?" Gently, so as not to disturb the tranquility of her friend, who was most certainly arranging an unusual surprise of some sort, she cracked open the door. The sun, high overhead, washed the interior of the mailbox with pure, hot, golden light, light strong enough so that even an elderly woman with miserable bifocal lenses could not mistake that which was within. The elderly woman was dumbfounded to discover that which was within was not at all what was expected.

Instead of her friend, a sweet-faced toy bear smiling a toothy mischievous welcome, there was something altogether different. Practically filling the entire insides of the mailbox, was the magnificently impenetrable web of an extremely large, many-eyed, affronted-looking spider.

Pots of Crème

Get as many pots as can be managed before Victoria returns from the bathroom and pour them full to the brim from the carton labeled Heavy Cream or Whipping Cream. Secret these about the house, allowing the cream to thicken, and then slurp slurp slurp and chew chew chew to your heart's content.

Chapter 7

Naturally, Fire

The spider remained motionless. Victoria was as a statue. Neither blinked. For fully one minute the impasse continued. Gingerly, her intention to cause as little alarm as possible, Victoria angled a shaking hand up from underneath, and then with just the tips of her garden-dirty fingers, swung the mailbox door shut with a bang. She felt quite faint. "That dashed sun!" she murmured. The post to which the mailbox was affixed offered her the nearest support. She clung there as to a life-raft, floating asea with blurred vision, swimming in and out on the wash of shallow breaths. Time stood still. When roused at last by a prolonged cool breeze, the human lurched away and tottered stiffly back through the gate into the sanctuary of her own garden.

"Tea. I must have tea." After giving herself a thorough wash up and cool down, she was seated at her immense kitchen table, calm and collected once more with a cup of steaming herbal tea braced with lemon and a larger than usual dollop of honey. "I don't have time right now to give in to poignant recollections," she rebuked herself, "of those happier times when I was not so pitiable an object. I must gather my wits about me."

She sipped her tea. "I must not have read the notices closely enough. I don't believe they were at all about the grass and weeds, but most probably were about that spider in the mailbox. No wonder I haven't heard from my old friends lately." She acknowledged the reasonableness of the mailman's refusal to deliver her mail under those circumstances, but, "Why couldn't he have just told me? I was standing right there in person, larger than life."

There was no accounting for other people's actions. She at least would not have to assume responsibility for that! Based on years of wisdom acquired the hard way, she was easily prepared to dismiss that vexing and inexplicable government employee from her mind. However, she could not do so without first imagining the scene. That innocent mailman, opening the mailbox day after day, for how many days? and being confronted by that malevolent spider.

"When he saw me at the gate, he must have assumed I had come out to remove it! No wonder he was so resentful!" Suddenly, she shook with laughter. "Whew! I should be sharing this with Kitty, wherever she is. This would delight her no end. That rude and silent man. The gigantic spider in the mailbox. Lucky for him he only has to deal with the one in the mailbox, since he doesn't know about the one in the garden shed..." Something troubling caused her to stop her gleeful imagining. She now remembered Kitty's prolonged absence.

"I'd almost forgotten. Now where could she be? What was it she said?" A vague recollection, of an angry and cunning Miss

Kitty. Something about matches! Something about a promise to burn...!

Though weakened by her traumatic recent experience, the frail woman leapt to her feet and bolted out the back door. Her worst fears were confirmed when she caught the smell of burning, and then almost immediately the sight of smoke, and tongues of fire licking the sides of the shed. "Oh no! Kitty! What have you done?"

The garden hose was hanging on its hook by the back door but disconnected from the water tap. It took a mighty effort to shake out the stiff rubber coils and connect it properly, but then it was done, and a stream of water splashed over the shed, dousing the flames and sending towering plumes of smoke high in the air. Victoria coughed a little as she circled the singed grass and blackened building. The insides were as dank and fetid as if nothing had happened. In reality, she had done more damage with the water than was caused by the fire. In only one small area was there any evidence at all that an arsonist had been at work. Several spent matches, a smear of black soot, some scorched ornamental grass, and the burnt places along the bottom were the only evidence there had been a near-disaster. Even the billowing smoke was now rapidly dissipated.

A contemptuous voice came from behind her. "You needn't have gone to all that trouble with the hose, Victoria. I've been trying for ages and the best I could do was to scorch it a little. I recommend you buy new matches. Yours are damp. Still, it was almost enough, I think, to teach that monster a lesson."

Victoria could not believe her ears, and yet when she dared to turn her head, there sat the smug little toy bear, pontificating coldly from her perch atop the upturned wheelbarrow.

Pickles in Shoes

Find a very stout pair of Victoria's old shoes (ones in the back of the closet are best), pack in cucumbers, some salt, sugar, dillweed and enough vinegar to cover. Test daily, taking just small bites around the edges, till they are done, then announce, "Who wants pickles?" and serve.

Chapter 8

Corn, Swimming in Butter

Of course some sort of punishment must be meted out. There was no question about that. Such recklessness of action, such depraved disregard for safety, could not go without something more severe than a simple scolding, however pointed and heartfelt. Kitty was an expert at deflecting Victoria's many efforts at a good talking-to away from herself, and so she had shrugged indifferently upon noticing the expression darkening Victoria's face with shades of red and even tinges of purple.

"Yes, yes, I know what you are thinking. I was wrong, I admit it. But...do you smell that? Pray, do smell that!" the bear insisted. "Almost like a roast beef, on a spit. I wonder..."

Victoria's features hardened, turning more purple-black. Kitty saw at once that her friend refused to be diverted. The crime was much too serious to permit the woman acknowledging that she also did indeed notice a very intriguing odor coming from the direction of the shed. Victoria suddenly realized that she had once again, quite without being fully aware of it, skipped another meal, and consequently was very hungry. Her mouth watered. She brushed roughly at the wetness accumulating in the corners of her lips with the backs of her hands.

"Must I remind you once again that we are not hermits, sequestered away upon the top of an isolated mountain, but are instead living here on an ordinary street in an ordinary small city, amongst ordinary members of ordinary society? Even if those ordinary citizens are the same ones I now personally know to be justified in accusing us of living in a state of precarious balance? What if someone had seen the smoke, smelled the fire, and called the fire department? What if the shed had gone up like a torch and engulfed the house? Kitty, you really must..."

The bear was brazen. "Tut tut! Surely, my dear, you are making a mountain of a molehill!" She wrinkled her snout with displeasure. "The house has not been burnt! Not even near to. No one has been harmed, especially not that nasty spider; and if you will just bend down a little, just a very little, from your inconvenient height to take a closer look, you will see that there has been very little damage done to your property either."

Having been shushed, Victoria gnawed her lips in silent resentment. If Kitty was waiting a reply from the human, her wait was in vain. The bear continued on unperturbed. "Perhaps a coat of paint will do the trick. You are handy with a brush, as am I. We shall soon make short work of it. That should conceal the blackened places. Or, I must say, I do rather like your scheme of allowing the grass to grow so high, as you have been doing! So clever of you! Or perhaps if we were to–well, why didn't I think of it before? What say you to planting a few ears of corn...?"

Stung at last into speaking, Victoria drew herself up in supreme indignation. "Do not," she stated distinctly, "attempt to turn your heedless act of vandalism into a scheme for corn! Really! How shameless are you? I have already spoken plainly to you regarding that subject. I am not a farmer, and neither are you. We shall continue to purchase our food at the grocery store, like normal people, and will not entertain any more notions of plowing under my beautiful and sophisticated garden into fields of coarse vegetables, or riding tractors across the lower forty acres, or swillin' the hogs, or..." She was prepared to go on indefinitely.

"Imagine it!" Kitty's eyes gleamed, swimming with tears of longing. "Sweet corn, dripping with melted butter, lolling about in pools of melted butter, crunchy sweetness, salty dripping..."

"Those things are now forbidden me, as you very well know," Victoria coldly reminded her. "I cannot in any case loll about in pools of melted butter."

"The corn. I mean to say the ears of corn swimming in melted butter."

"That is all very well for you, Kitty, but unless I am mistaken, and knowing you as I do, you were also imagining yourself lolling in the pools of butter, which to my way of thinking is the sole reason for your desire to grow acres of corn.

Be honest now Kitty, the corn is only secondary to your lusting after pools of melted butter."

Tempers were heating up. Much more had been said than the situation required. Voices had been raised. Neither female was prepared to yield, though both were salivating to at least one's discomposure. The wiping of lips was completed surreptitiously behind the folds of lace-edged hankies, demurely under the pretense of dabbing at beads of perspiration. This was entirely within the bounds of common etiquette, since it was a hot day.

Victoria could not help taking one last swipe. "You would almost certainly stubbornly demand your corn raw in any case. The melted butter would congeal and turn lumpy. Now if you were to boil the corn, hot corn on the cob…"

"I prefer to take my chances, my dear, with raw corn in its natural state even with lumpy butter." That was all there was to be said on the subject for the bear refused to allow that mushy cooked corn with all the crunch boiled out of it was fit for consumption, even by humans.

You, Dear Reader, will see by the success of this tactic, that the bear's skill in diverting attention away from the subject at hand was impressive. For quite ten minutes, the woman forgot all about the execution of the criminal act, until Kitty drew her attention to it herself by insisting that just a paltry few rows of corn here, a modest field of tomatoes there, a mere acre or two of potatoes there (such fun to dig up, like a treasure hunt!), and of course, a few dozen chickens ensconced in a comfortable coop near the ancient Concord grape vines.

"Chickens, one has heard, are more than willing to provide eggs, and if luck were to have it, perhaps an opera singer as well. Were they not acquainted with one operatic chicken? Might there be another such to be found amongst common hens? Well, that would be just the thing, and so very economical, too."

Victoria's mind turned back from these delights with a thud of disbelief to the atrocity performed upon the garden shed. "We must deal with this immediate and disgusting act of violence against property, now, Miss Katherine, and put your bucolic fantasies to rest. I shall not be diverted again. There will be no further adventures with fire, whether you feel they are justified by circumstances or not, Retaliation, revenge, rage; these incendiary motivations must not compel you to take actions destructive to our home, for such it is for both of us, Kitty. We have already experienced water damage, at your hands, we must not toy with fire. Do I have the assurance I require, that you will control yourself?"

That bear gazed blankly at the human's face. A soft snore escaped, fluttering her oh, so expressive rigid plastic lips. It was too much. The human stomped away indignantly. Duty compelled a swift return and a not very gentle retrieval. Her companion woke with a snort, limbs flailing, to find herself removed from her perch atop the wheelbarrow, caged within Victoria's unforgiving icy fingers, and plopped unceremoniously down inside Barton Cottage. Kitty's home now rested within Victoria's living room, where it was cozier and more convenient for all.

The friends were reunited at Victoria's kitchen table shortly afterwards. Tea, that most soothing of beverages, was required, and slid easily down their eager throats. Nuggets of tender ham bound together by cheese-thickened cream and spooned atop crisp crackers made a satisfying meal accompanied by quartered grape tomatoes sprinkled with salt. The bear had insisted upon over-sugaring the translucent red tea filling the pale porcelain cups and dousing it with thick cream. "We have had a trying morning," she remarked with smug complacency, "What with the stressful weeding and the fire and all. We must pamper ourselves in whatever way we find necessary. Or to hand."

By way of these pretty sentiments she felt free to indulge herself in a gluttonous dessert of two whole ripe strawberries dipped in sugar, though the fruit was larger than her head, and seven of the famous butter cookies, which are molded in the shape of human mittened-hands, unbaked of course, being composed of nothing but butter and sugar.

Her larger and therefore more usually-sized friend nibbled her own share of the sweet goodies, while gazing in hollow-eyed abstraction at the bleakness of recent events and the lack of immediate resolution. Thus engaged, she failed to notice Miss Kitty boldly gnawing upon the sugar-encrusted edges of her own share of the butter cookies.

Her fingers moved automatically over the empty plate but were quickly brushed aside by an industrious bear scouting for crumbs. "You are...this behavior is most inelegant my dear. Your skirt! I say! Your skirt is bunched up around your knees! Most shocking! Please have a care. Most shocking! I say, do not you find the butter-hand cookies to be less toothsome than usual? They seem to be...I am finding them...somewhat lacking in that crunchy crust. I am so very fond of that crunchy crust, as you well know."

Kitty pretended not to hear these comments. Her selective hearing was surpassed only by her selective understanding. She gave one final lick to the already shiny clean surfaces of the porcelain plates before sinking back in blissful contentment.

Her eyelids drooped. "I fear I must leave you now, Victoria dear. I have a good many small tasks awaiting me at home: tidying up, correspondence with old friends...and other things. Things to do. If you do not mind, I shall be on my way. Perhaps later, if you insist, we may continue this...this engrossing conversation."

Victoria could not have stopped her if she tried. With all four paws twinkling over the polished wood of the table, the bear vanished in an instant, down the ladder-like rungs of the chair to the floor and out of the kitchen into the living room. A brief scramble could be heard, and then a mild oath, as the tiny bear hoisted herself up over the two inch high threshold into her cottage, then all was silence.

"You are right, Kitty dear. I could use a nap myself," Victoria called after her.

However, instead of napping, which was much the safer course, the woman wandered forlornly out the back door into the garden. Late afternoon shadows streaked the tousled grasses with interesting stripes in subdued colors. Birds twittered in alarm and started up when she approached, small animals rustled in the un-raked leaves and dashed across her path, and more than one adolescent spider drag-lined across her face. A snake gamely slithered overtop her shoe, disappearing down a sizeable hole eroded between the stones of a weed-choked rock wall.

"This is becoming ridiculous!" The garden had indeed degenerated, to a degree much greater than she had ever before allowed herself to notice. Up till this moment, the woman's selective observation was surpassed only by her selective blindness. The once, some might say, overly-manicured, too-disciplined garden, was now a much more comfortable habitat for the creatures of the wild; but as for civilized creatures, well that was a different matter.

The woman noticed a jagged stub of a branch protruding from an ancient maple tree. "That, I can take care of at least!" she muttered. The bedraggled old tea-party hat was located under a bush and pulled firmly down over her ears. She chuckled a little at the thought of Kitty being almost able to recognize it from all those long-ago tea parties. The pile of rusty tools she had rescued from the shed were leant together in an untidy heap against the wood fence. She grasped the tree pruning hook in unsteady fingers, while carefully bracing her feet and positioning herself where she might have the best leverage. "Safety first!" Still, for all her precautions and past experience, nonetheless she too was rusty, and greatly overestimated the force required. She threw her weight into it. At her sharp tug, the dried-out branch cracked cleanly off the trunk and sailed through the air quite like a spear tossed by an aborigine of wild plains, or a whaler upon tossing seas, or a warrior woman battling flies, coming to impact squarely with her forehead!

"OOH!" she moaned. The spar of dead wood stuck where it had penetrated for just a second before falling to the ground. The elderly woman blinked away the alternating bright white starbursts and black spirals twinkling in her eyes. She gingerly felt the place where she had been struck, encountering there a rapid swelling as well as three sharp splinters of rotted wood embedded in her scalp. She shuddered as she pulled these bits from the wound. With blood now flowing freely over her face, Victoria tottered into the house, fell without an oath or murmur onto the couch, and abruptly took a nap.

Ham and Biscuits

Thinly slice the saltiest piece of ham you can find. Do not be too fussy over whether it is cooked or raw, since ham is certainly safe for most of us to eat. Put layers of thin slices on a heavily buttered biscuit, add some grated Swiss cheese, and do not rely on good manners to tell you how to proceed!

Chapter 9

Injuries to the Head and Hand

"I wish," began Victoria, "I wish…" Her wishes were left unspoken for the time being, since she was not quite yet capable of articulation.

A growly voice near her left ear pronounced grimly, "If wishes were horses… well, you know the rest of that old chestnut!"

"No, I don't. And neither do you."

The bear wisely kept her own wishes and opinions to herself, for her human friend was in that irritable state between recovery and coma, so annoyingly drawn-out to the patiently on-looking caregiver, but so necessary to the achievement of full sensibility. That it was the next morning, that Victoria had slept through the afternoon and evening and all night long on the couch instead of in her own bed, were two things the human had been able to ascertain. She knew she had been at it for some time, drifting into and out of consciousness, raving wildly about spears and spiders, and dwelling most unpleasantly upon 'crimes' committed by a certain toy bear.

In any case the morning proved her to be a much pleasanter object at which to look. Kitty, ever desiring to be useful, had been busy during the night while the human slept, industriously licking away all the dried blood, and chewing reflectively upon the succulent clots matting her dear friend's hair, till all was smooth and dry and the skin was pink again. What Victoria's wishes might be upon discovery of her nurse's unusual bed-side technique was best left to the imagination.

At present the woman was only aware that her head was thumping most maddeningly in time to the beating of her heart, drowning out rational conversation. She was aware of a desire to communicate something important but was as yet unable to do more than eye the toy bear with displeasure before falling once again into an unquiet nap.

When fully restored to herself, and after a good wash-up and with the head wounds cleansed in the more usual way, and with a piece of sticking plaster protecting the worst of the holes, the woman turned her aching brain to pondering multiple problems. Least important of the problems was the lack of blood from her wound. Head wounds, she had read somewhere, bleed alarmingly, but this wound had been remarkably tidy.

She examined the rather frighteningly large swelling in the bathroom mirror. "What an odd shade of purple. But no blood, and the edges of the wounds are free of scabs. Perhaps I'm anemic. I shall have to increase my iron consumption. The brown pill." Her shudders were by now so frequent an event, they went un-remarked.

Most important, and the problem nagging relentlessly was the matter of the garden, which seemed inexplicably to have turned against her. "I am not as diligent as in the past; however, I do not believe I have been that remiss, or for such a length of time which might have permitted things to deteriorate so far." This last thought revealed, more plainly than anything, Dear Reader, that delusions indeed are one of the neglected side effects of head wounds, for as any conscientious gardener or even the average non-gardening citizen will tell you, when nature will, it almost must run amok. If in possession of her right mind, Victoria would have known this to be a universal truth.

A consultation with a friend was in order. Kitty had run off after making sure the human was fully restored to her senses, and there were no more appetizingly salty meaty clotted bloody tidbits to be had. Victoria called, "Kitty? Kitty where are you?"

"I am here, Victoria, dear, at home."

The bear was industriously rootling around in her pantry hidden behind the ten-step staircase. This was a room long concealed from the human's sight until brought uncomfortably to her knowledge the previous year, when she found herself actually within it! Powers beyond comprehension had been unleashed during or perhaps by, the woman's cerebral accident, resulting in her seeming to be reduced in size to a hair under four inch. Now at her normal, though gigantically impractical height of five feet and four inches, the human had found a practical solution to the problem. In order to confidently avoid having unpleasant surprises foisted upon her, she had resorted to technology.(The floor-to-ceiling towers of her home-baked cookies which Kitty had purloined, concealing for her own use, was one such unpleasantness.)A long-handled, angled mechanic's mirror seemed designed expressly for the purpose of spying into the places she could not now fit. Kitty found the mirror a welcome and elegant solution, for though the loss of the companionship of her height-equalized friend was still a source of the bitterest regrets, the bear was charity itself in acknowledging the obvious; that her dear Victoria must miss indeed the hidden delights of Barton Cottage. Who wouldn't?

Victoria gave herself up to the luxury of a lay-down upon her less-than-comfortable overstuffed sofa. With her head propped up on a fat squishy pillow, she was within arm's reach and direct eye-line of her friend's cottage, and able with small effort to see into all the rooms and peer into the darkest corners with the aid of the mirror. The arrangement, with Kitty's house moved to her living room, was made possible by Lily and her burly husband, and one for which Victoria chided herself for not having discovered sooner. All those years crouched cross-legged on the floor in the cold attic, or the months spent twisting about on the hard bench in the hall upstairs, before actually being able to visit the rooms in person, though at Kitty-size. "How conventional and foolish I am," she chuckled, "when I could have been reclining all along at my leisure in my own living room." And no scandal accompanied the arrangement, since no one of a regulation human-size came in person to visit or condemn her in ever so long.

Now she recalled the reason for her interest in Kitty's whereabouts. She made a minor adjustment to the mirror but was unable to ascertain exactly what it was the bear was doing. "What, pray tell, are you about?" she asked a little defensively, for she had just had a trying experience.

"Oh, you know, things. And other things." the bear muttered indistinctly.

As usual, this kind of foolishness drew a startled exclamation from the only too knowledgeable human. Kitty, Victoria knew better than anyone, loved to chat, so long as the conversation was within the limits of civilized discourse, on any subject, of her choosing, and almost at the level of monologue, when excited by her own witty observations and insights. An unwillingness to hold forth on a subject about "things" brought implications of the direst sort.

"Why, whatever can you find to be so engaging, you have not a moment to spare for conversation with a friend? Much needed conversation too." The mirror was utilized with more vigor.

Towers of purloined Christmas cookies filling the hidden space under the stairs was one thing. This was another matter altogether. Quicker than thought, the human thrust her hand in and around the secret cupboard where she blindly latched onto a startled and outraged Kitty, dragging her squirming with fury into the light. Before Victoria could remove her hand to safety, the bear had chomped down on a finger with murderous intent.

"OOH!" Victoria screamed. Her attacker fell from the injured hand to the carpeted living room floor, where she gathered herself up and proceeded to stomp indignantly as only a four inch tall toy bear can stomp.

Stolen Things

We all know for a fact that this is true: a stolen thing is ever so much tastier than anything that is just handed over like fodder to a tame cat. Try it for yourself. Take a bite of cheese stolen from the Cheese-board and then try eating a tiny sliver doled out by a friend. "Oh, thank you so much! No, no more for me. This is plenty!" Wear your biggest fake smile.

Chapter 10

A + B = C

An ominous calm descended like a wet black blanket over the living room. The angry swishing of Kitty's stiffly starched tea gown against the fibers of the carpet was the only sound piercing the dullness. To lower herself to the bear's level, to remonstrate in anger, to demand apologies that would not be forthcoming, was to stoop to folly, for Victoria knew only too well the scene that must ensue. And so she remained quite silently in control of herself, binding the injured digit in a handkerchief, and blinking back tears of outrage.

Her voice trembling with suppressed passion, the bear was the first to speak. "Shall you be taking it into your head to attack me once more, dear Victoria? Or have you quite exhausted your apparently limitless stores of malice, for the present?"

The quivering of dammed-up rage in Victoria's voice equaled that of her friend. "It is not I, as you very well know, my dear Kitty, who bears the onus of attacker, for I am the one nursing a bloody stump of a finger."

"A matter of sheer animal instinct, a reaction, produced purely as a response to provocation! A, plus B, equals C." The bear trembled with wild animal indignation. "A finger..." Here, her voice shook so with emotion, she needed a moment to control its quavering. "A monstrous, humongous finger accompanied by at least three others, as well as an abominably pretentious opposable thumb, used in an assault upon my person whilst within my own sovereign home, engaged upon my own lawful business."

At this point, all decorum was lost. The two friends battled; voices raised. The squabbling went on beyond good breeding or common sense, and so, as discretion is the better part of wisdom, we shall take this opportunity to turn our eyes and ears away from disharmony and rancor in order to elevate ourselves by contemplating subjects on a higher plane. Let us, for example, examine our surroundings in the living room. A beautiful and functional room, of good proportions, paneled in dark old wood. Victoria has furnished the space with her collection of elegant yet functional chairs, occasional tables, sofas, and writing desks. A room meaninglessly crowded perhaps, for seldom are the chairs sat upon or the tables utilized. Though all of these objects, beautifully clean and empty, still bear faint evidence of water damage from a long-ago Kitty-inspired flooding disaster...however, let us not forget ourselves by revisiting old grievances, but confine ourselves instead to thoughts of beauty and harmony. Many of the walls are covered with shelves holding a considerable library of expensively bound books, some of which have been read, and many of which are sprinkled between their pages with crumbs of buttery shortcake and crystals of sugar. The parquet floor is bedecked with hand-loomed imported rugs, and a high-mantled fireplace protected with a worked-iron screen, is bathed in the soft afternoon light streaming through a large floor-to-ceiling glass door opening onto the flagstone patio leading to the garden outside.

When calm had been restored, greased as usual by the liberal application of large quantities of tea heavily creamed and sugared, and a more than usual quantity of hard biscuits chosen expressly for the maximum display of gnashing teeth, Victoria was forced to defend her uncharacteristic assault with an explanation. This she did with succinct energy.

"You were flicking a lighter. A cigarette lighter you have gotten from God knows where. I will not have it in my house. The points you claim in self-defense, if I am to understand you: that you were in your own house, and the lighter did not even work, are immaterial. Your house is in my house, and I will not depend upon happenstance or mechanical failure to protect my home and property and even my life. You have already proven your sterling aptitude with water, my dear, and now you have introduced fire. The matter must end here and now."

Kitty had the grace then to blush and cover her face with her paws. This touching scene was one recommended by past experience to bring her friend round in a jiffy. The "cute factor" Victoria was wont to call it. Advanced age had softened the human's temper as well as her faculties: though excusing bad behavior because of a "cute" moment would have been unthinkable to the rational Victoria of old, fondly making excuses for her friend, now, was commonplace. However, due to the extremity of risk posed by Kitty's latest interest, the cuteness of the bear's calculated gesture failed to bring about the desired response. The human glared, stating that she, as mistress of the house, would stand for no further funny business.

At the toy's refusal to acknowledge any wrongdoing or promise in the future to control her actions, Victoria became quite enraged. "I will pack you up in a box which I will tightly wrap around with tape and send you off into outer-space, Kitty, I really shall. You have frightened me past all bearing." Immediately, realizing the truly awfulness of this threat, the woman clamped down on her tongue. "Oh my Dear," she uttered faintly. "Please forgive me. That was unworthy of me, and I do apologize most sincerely."

"I should say so, Victoria! Imagine thinking such a thing. You should not have threatened a human friend in this manner." Kitty was shocked indeed. She attempted to camouflage her distress by swiping vigorously at imaginary specks of dust on her apron, so vigorously, in fact, the ancient, long-neglected apron strings tore off and the apron itself hung limply from the bear's claw. She stared at it uncomprehending.

Victoria took a very deep breath. "You are right. You are quite right. I have no excuse. There is no excuse. Know that this unpardonable error shall never come between us again. You have my solemn promise."

On that note, the woman rose with stiff dignity. The toy bear was sitting all a 'heap on the carpet just outside of Barton Cottage. The insult quite forgot, she had taken to playing with a bit of lint fallen from the torn apron, puffing and blowing to see how high it would go. "I meant to mention, dear one, there is the matter of that hat...that tea hat with the roses..."

Victoria pretended not to hear. She was satisfied that several things had been accomplished: she herself had committed a grievous faux-pas, for which she had apologized, the apology had been accepted, and she had impressed upon her friend the dreadfulness of her arsonist actions. With the nonfunctioning cigarette lighter (wherever had she found such a thing?) safely tucked away in a locked cupboard, Kitty severely chastised, she turned her mind to other problems.

Carrots in Sweet Things

Do not ever put vegetables in cakes. Or any sweets. Period.

Chapter 11

Blood on The Wall

"As I recall," Victoria muttered to herself, "one of the things mentioned in that lengthy notice of improvements, which was eaten up by Kitty, that in order to bring my home up to code, I must prominently display an address number at the front large enough for it to be seen from outer space. Well, that is one problem to which I can attend with relative ease."

There were many cans of paint lining a shelf in the basement, most dried out till they rattled when shook, some too thick to be practical, and only a few liquid enough to coat a paintbrush. Of these, one was a shocking scarlet, one a daring turquoise-blue, and the last a dull olive-green with grains of sand thickening it. "I really cannot remember what these were used for. As far as I can tell, I have never seen any of them." This last statement was a clear sign of forgetfulness, for surely the turquoise was the same paint with which she once, long ago, desecrated Kitty's home, mistaking in the dim light of the attic, turquoise-blue for gray.

Her house displayed attractive touches of nature's colors, especially in the entranceway closest to the street; a cheerful, red-leafed Burning Bush, a smattering of yellow, orange, and even purple flowers amongst all the greenery, and of course the bright blues and pinks of the hydrangeas. The house itself was of glistening white wood above the stone foundation. The woman walked thoughtfully out to the gate and turned for a look.

"With the coming of winter, all these colors will be gone. It will all be quite dreary and monotonous, faded to whites and grays, in the dim gray winter light. Too depressing! I believe, yes, I believe with the right color I shall be able to fulfill my civic requirements as well as brighten things up a bit!"

When she returned to the house, it was to find Kitty lying prone just inside the door on the doormat on the very spot where she had blown her lint-ball. Not yet tired of her sport, she puffed it up again and again into the air, over and over, exclaiming in annoyance, "Oh, bother!" when the elusive bit of fluff now went vanishing down the hall on the gust of wind from the opened door.

"Kitty, my dear, I almost stepped on you! You are just the person I wanted to see. Come along, come along now and leave off your game. We are compelled to do something artistic."

The bear skidded to a stop and ran back. "I must say, I am intrigued, Victoria. Shall you once again attempt the seven-layer cake? That technique has long escaped you. Or perhaps it is something savory you have in mind?"

"No, no, you are quite mistaken there. This is not about food, but something functional and decorative; a house project." The bear's plastic features fell. "I will require your advice, you know, as you are the expert in the art of decoration, as well as cake-baking, while I definitely am not."

Mollified, Kitty lit up, dashing off to Barton Cottage to retrieve her spectacles. Though these spectacles, made for her by the Butler many years ago and fashioned out of twisted wire, held no glass lenses within their delicate framework, she believed they enhanced the appearance of intelligence, making her look rather more like her human friend. When Victoria complained about her bifocals, Kitty did as well.

Out they trooped to the front of the house. Kitty's advice, though often unasked for, often overbearing, and always impertinent, was generally practical and useful. (Lady Catherine, indeed!) Victoria acknowledged as much, for on this occasion especially, she had not the slightest idea how to proceed. Together they outlined the approximate dimensions of the numbers, on the appropriate spot a little to the left of the stone column of the porch, above the bushes growing there, and within plain sight of the street. Kitty, in a generosity of spirit, refrained from pushing her preference for the turquoise paint, not wishing to be accused of harboring any nagging resentment or feelings of vengeance. But she was clearly overjoyed when Victoria chose the scarlet, for secretly that had been her first choice.

Victoria painted diligently, making the first number almost one foot high, and being careful of drips. Kitty, perched on the limb of an ornamental tree, was supposed to be spotting the operation, guiding and directing the human hand in case Victoria should go off course, but having lost interest, was instead lolling back among the leaves, gazing skyward, shouting out when she spotted humorous cloud formations, and optimistically hunting for rainbows. That, the human later assured her, was why things went so badly wrong.

The first foot-high number was plainly visible to anyone not immediately blinded by it, that much was certain. The second was slightly shorter, the third and fourth shorter yet, till the fifth was roughly half the size of the first. They also ran uphill. Aghast, the human and the bear examined the effect, heads tilted to the left in identical postures of disbelief. As if things weren't bad enough, the thick red paint unaccountably began to run, and ran, and ran, and there was no stopping it. Victoria made a frantic effort to wipe the initial drips with a turpentine-soaked rag but could not contain the rivers of red seeping steadily down the wall.

"Why Victoria! I had no idea!" Kitty exclaimed. "It looks...it looks...just like blood!" Her delight was obvious. "Like oozing drops of blood! I like it! I love it! This proclaims to the world that we denizens of this home, sequestered inmates behind these walls, are not to be trifled with. Not at all! Hooray! I congratulate you!" The human said nothing. What was there to say?

Pepperoni

Love love love love love love love love salty oily spicy fatty greasy delicious pepperoni especially when the chunk under my bed has aged a bit. Love love it.

Chapter 12

The Emily Bronte Method of Dog Training, Again

"Is it Deja vu?" The scene was one of curiously familiar significance. Victoria's heart pounded. Kitty was heard to be rooting around in the hidden closet under the stairs inside Barton Cottage. "Am I losing my mind? Is time repeating itself?" The woman sank down upon the couch and stared into the cottage windows. When that revealed nothing, she resolutely grasped the long-handled mechanic's mirror and shoved it without ceremony into the secret recesses of the house.

The mirror displayed the backside of the toy bear practically burrowing into the slanted-roofed space under the stairs through piles of her junk, and then suddenly standing erect and bumping her head on the low ceiling, with a triumphant cry of discovery. "Aha! I knew it must be somewhere, and I was right!"

The something she had found was waved excitedly. The bear backed out into her living room and bumped into the mirror. "Excuse me," she murmured absentmindedly, rushing to show her gigantically looming friend the object grasped in her paw; a butterfly net, much tattered, missing its handle, and extremely dusty. "I've found what I was looking for! So satisfying! Will you excuse me please, Victoria, I have some netting to do. Some repairs to this device must be undertaken without delay. We shall have a good, long, chat later, if you don't mind." With hardly a glance at the woman, or waiting for a reply, the bear dragged the net to her favorite chair under the good, strong, lamp, with the rattan work basket tucked on the floor beside it, and humming softly, drew out her needles and began to make repairs.

The woman was not so easily stifled, nor would she permit herself to be dismissed in such a condescending manner. "My dear Kitty, I simply must speak with you. I have to confess I have been letting things go around here, that much was made evident when that mailman refused to deliver my mail. And just now, the condition of the garden shed, and the variety and quantity of wild animals making themselves comfortable, and the outrageousness of the plants! There are weeds, if you can believe it, higher than even my head. I am certain that you, on your solitary forays throughout the garden must have noticed how overgrown everything has become. How have you failed to recall it to my attention?"

"Oh, this is too much!" Kitty was brusque. "Please do not reflect your human carelessness upon me! I have not neglected my concerns!"

Victoria cast down her eyes. "Yes, yes, you are quite right. I was hoping to parcel out the blame. It makes it easier to ask for help when friends feel they share some responsibility. Also, I am afraid of that spider."

The bear paused in her industrious netting. "I shall give help, gladly, Victoria, when it is required and sought after. However, you must know that I have my own methods. You may not be in agreement."

Victoria began heatedly, "Are we talking about setting things on fire again?"

Kitty energetically shushed her. "I was about to inform you, hasty one, that I have come up with a little plan. I realize not all my methods are to your liking, but I can assure you that this one will be."

"I'm all ears."

"No, dear, you are not. We should not have quite so many disagreements if that were true. My plan, if you are quite composed, concerns this very same spider. There now! I propose that we tame this ferocious animal, using the Emily Bronte method of dog training, and make her our ally rather than our enemy." The toy bear beamed.

"Are you serious?"

Kitty fluffed out her always voluminous skirts. "Of course I am serious. The Bronte method will require some small adjustments, but on the whole, I think it is an elegant plan, which will solve your problem with the spider in the mailbox, as well as the problem with the other spider in the shed, and the half dozen other problems in other areas, of which you are presently unaware."

The woman was taken aback. "What? I am certain there can be no more than one such gigantic spider, Kitty! One that must be traveling between the mailbox and the shed. Surely there cannot be more than one."

Kitty smiled at the foolishness of her friend. "That is sheer wishful thinking, and you know it, as well as an alarming lack of knowledge about the territoriality of arachnids. There are three spider sisters of which I am certain, and probably dozens more. Spiders lay eggs in the hundreds. After consuming as many as she can, a valuable source of nutrition, the mother spider sinks into a torpor and therefore there are always a lucky few of her children who manage to escape to live to see another day." She thoughtfully tapped her front teeth with a blunted claw. "Yes, that one, and I am reminded of, I can say with certainty, there is evidence of at least a dozen spiders in this immediate vicinity."

Victoria was struck dumb. She knew better than to question Kitty's statistics. Knowing the bear as she did, over such a lengthy period of time, the woman felt certain Kitty had indeed made a rigorous investigation and might therefore have exaggerated by only 50% for her own devious purposes. Even at 50%, however, that left 6 of the monstrous spiders on the loose and hidden within the grounds of her…. A terrible thought caused her blood pressure to rise. A vein pulsed dangerously in her head, causing the almost-healed wound to throb. "Kitty," she panted, "please do tell…"

"Calm yourself my dear. I know exactly what it is you are so eager to ask, and you may rest assured that there are no spiders in your house! They are all confined to the gardens, front and back, under the trees, and in burrows underground."

Victoria sighed with relief. Again, she harbored no doubts of Kitty's veracity. The bear tolerated spiders no better than she; despite any wild schemes that might be churning in her untamed-animal breast, Kitty would report if one of the creatures had breached the sanctity of the home she shared with the human.

Bug Salad

Find the fattest bugs you can and coax them into your salad with promises of good things to eat. Then go right ahead and eat them. They won't mind, and if they do, we shan't know it because bugs are that dumb and do not even have a proper language. Add salt.

Chapter 13

Alarming Reports Coming In

Lily, The (former) Butler, called her mother long distance. She chatted comfortably about the baby and her husband, the new house, new country, customs, and the language barrier, breezily nattering on before realizing Victoria was unaccountably silent. "How are things going with you then? Is everything all right back there? How's Kitty?"

"Oh, she's fine. Just fine. I'll tell her you asked after her."

This response could not quite satisfy the Butler's curiosity. Long sensitized to nuance, the unspoken shades of meaning in her mother's voice, she felt the hair rise on the back of her neck. Much too casually, yet unable to conceal a high-pitched note of hysteria, the younger woman asked, "Well, tell me, what's going on then? No, don't tell me, let me guess! Kitty has flooded the house again, hasn't she?"

"Oh, no! No, of course not. It's not flooding, silly! It's fire this time, I'm afraid, but no harm done. Well, no harm done, so far. With Kitty there's no telling! I'm keeping my fingers crossed; all my fingers, and toes too, that she's given over that idea. And I have securely locked up that cigarette lighter! I'm assuming it's one of yours, since I do not smoke, and I didn't know that you did either, so thank you very much for that! One of your secret rebellions, I suppose. No, you'll be relieved to hear, as I was, that she's moved on from fire, and you'll laugh when I tell you, to her old Emily Bronte method of dog training. You might remember that; she called it the "Emily Bronte method of dog training" after something you read to her in a biography; well perhaps you won't remember that far back; anyway, she's using it on those gigantic spiders, if you can believe it, not dogs. It's putting my nerves through the wringer; I can tell you that!"

Victoria heard her daughter taking deep calming breaths before speaking, or squeaking rather, for her voice sounded pinched. "Maybe you should start at the beginning."

"Sorry. Not now. I'd love to catch up, but I really can't right now. In fact I'm a little rushed, since that mailman, although he's been AWOL for quite some time, might actually be here shortly and I need to stop him before he opens the mailbox again. I can't afford to have any really important letters just thrown down on the street like he's been doing, you know, though it's been quite some time since I've received any really important mail, anything I'd care to read; so I've hung a plastic bag underneath the box, and I want to make sure he uses it. That's the best I can think of till we can get that monster out of there. I absolutely refuse to run about setting things on fire, and so I'm forced to wait out Kitty's master plan. She keeps hatching these plans. So like her. I can't seem to be able to think clearly now...well, oh! Of course that's it, since I've had this head wound, you know! I may possibly be anemic. But, speaking of blood, I think the mailman, whenever he deigns to return, might be shocked! What if he suspects we've used actual blood on the numbers on the front of the house? As some sort of protest? Or irony? Oh well...I can't help it if he's that sensitive...he's so very strange... who knows what he might think? I've really got to run now! Kiss the baby for me!"

Lily hung up the phone with a thoughtful expression. Her husband, passing by with the baby in his arms noticed. "Is everything all right?" he asked.

Lily, now in full-Butler-alarm-mode, chewed her lip. "No. I'm not sure. No, no, I am sure. I am more than certain that everything is not all right. In fact, nothing seems to be right." She stopped in the center of the room, and counted upon her fingers: fire, monstrous spiders, mailmen, Emily Bronte-training method, plastic bags, head wound, blood...? She wandered across the room, picked up the phone directory and sank into a chair. "Let me think," she murmured. After a moment, she began placing calls.

Victoria's anticipation of the mailman's reaction was all for naught, for either he had no mail to deliver to this end of the cul-de-sac or was simply refusing to put himself through another wearisome encounter with a malignant spider and/or a deranged old woman, and so made no appearance at all.

"Well, I can hardly blame him," Victoria sighed. "There was probably no mail worth bothering with. I wonder if Lily took the hint about sending me a letter? She most certainly could send something now and then. A few pictures of the baby would be wonderful. He'll be walking before I see him again." A sound drew her attention to the hallway. She listened closely, for the sound of things on fire. "What would that sound like I wonder? A rushing? Like wind? I'd probably smell fire before I heard it."

Yes, definitely, something was being scraped along the wood floor. Not at all like her concept of what fire should sound like though, if anything recognizable, the sound was more like the scraping of hard plastic. The woman peeked around the doorway in time to see that the something looked like a small dog exiting the backdoor! Eyes burning with curiosity, she tiptoed rapidly along the hall carpet to the door, and then, scarcely breathing, peered through the glass pane out onto the flagstone patio. There she discovered something quite amazing, and yet, almost amazingly perfect, for her dear friend Miss Kitty was sitting astride the plastic Bideable horse, beaming up at her with pride!

Kitty could not wait till her friend was out the door, but in her eagerness, rushed on so that she was obliged to repeat herself. "Look," she said, "Look, Victoria, look! I've had the most marvelous idea! I've been so busy coming up with a plan, and this horse has agreed to help!" By the expression of stolid indifference on the horse's molded plastic countenance, this statement seemed one of Kitty's typical exaggerations. However,

Victoria was caught up in the brilliance of the idea and panted with the thrill of an unknown intrigue.

"Do not keep me in suspense, Dear One, but tell immediately. What is your plan?"

The bear leapt off the horse, only slightly disarranging her riding costume, and patted the plastic equine head soothingly. "Well, it had occurred to me, and I'm sure it must have occurred to you as well, that spiders, for all their ferocity of countenance and wildness of reputation, have one decided drawback to their personalities, which happily works to our favor: they are known to have an inordinate respect for authority. You, as well as I, must be aware of their keen deference to superior strength, size, and intelligence. It is a fact well known amongst those of our acquaintance accustomed to reading the encyclopedia. So, I remembered this noble steed sitting idle for much too long and coaxed him from his stall with promises of as many apples as he can eat. And with your blessing, and a fresh set of batteries I shall ride into the monsters' lairs upon this impressive beast, who has agreed to rear and flare his nostrils and snort most dangerously, and cow the spiders. When they are sufficiently subdued, I shall sweep them up into my net, imprison them somewhere, in a secure place, and tame them. Using the Emily Bronte method. You may, of course, help if help is required."

Victoria stared blankly. The sweeping, exhilarating image of Kitty dashing about on a rearing steed, plunging into harm's way to do battle with dangerous foes, had come down to earth with a thud. Imprisoning? Taming? What about flattening, or routing? What about smacking with a rolled-up magazine? Kitty beamed, awaiting her blessing. "A sound proposal. Let me think on it..."

"No, no, I insist! Now is the time for action! The time for thinking is past! Give me your word we shall act now!" The bear vibrated with the need for action. Even the horse had turned a disdainful eye upon the wishy-washy human. Victoria threw her hands in the air. Argument was unwise. The human hastened to hunt out and insert batteries into the belly of the trembling horse, making it incumbent upon herself to caution him that the batteries were not entirely fresh, having been borrowed from a small kitchen whisk.

Kitty discounted anything so anti-heroic as a warning, gathered her courage, repeating earnestly, "Now, is the time for action. Strike while the iron is hot. There are more than one of these spiders to contend with, and our time is running short. For all we know, eggs in the thousands may have been laid, and are already hatching."

"Oh! Yes, my dear, you may be right. To arms, then! Sally forth my brave little friend, the wind at your back, a noble steed to carry you..."

Kitty's store of patience had run out at this uncharacteristic verbosity, and she and the horse were off. "I should probably go along to make sure everything is as it should be," the woman muttered, "but I am so tired all of a sudden. I've done too much today." With that unpromising remark, she took herself off to the living room for a lay-down on the couch. While an epic battle raged outside her kitchen door, Victoria snored softly, and slept the sleep of the innocent.

If we are to make ourselves happy as well as carefree, we need not stoop to spying upon the events occurring in Victoria's shed, nor her mailbox. Let other pens describe tales of madness, let other tongues sing ballads of improbable heroism. Let us, gentle Readers, be content with knowing that deeds were done, acts were committed, and more heads than hearts were bruised.

Kitty's victory was assured. To reveal that the bear let it go to her head would do a disservice to head-possessors the world over. Victoria was silenced. The horse's role, which had been central and significant, was made much diminished in the bear's retelling, and he slunk off in disgust. His exit was less than heroic since, just as is to be expected in a world given over to ironic coincidence, the weakened batteries gave out, precisely as he was stomping off in a huff. Brought to an undignified halt, he pretended an exaggerated scholarly interest in the padded legs of an armchair, while sulking over his failure to obtain even a whiff of the promised apples.

Mayonnaise Mixed With Other Things

Put 1 cup of mayonnaise, (more if you can get it) chopped vegetables, cheese, meat, bugs, fruit, grass clippings, tree bark, literally anything, in a bowl and eat with a spoon.

Chapter 14

What's in the Attic?

"They are in the attic!" Kitty confided to her human friend. "I thought it much the best place for them."

There was no calming down the hysterics of an over-stimulated human. Visions of past ordeals involving Kitty and her projects: wild animals, including a vicious and destructive red squirrel invading her home; the demolition of the interior of that home by flooding at Kitty's hands, swamped the woman's mind and she would not be soothed.

When able at last to hear and therefore comprehend what the bear was proposing, she told herself it was not as bad as she first believed it to be. Indeed, it was now her default reaction to most Kitty-related situations, a slightly lowered recalibration of hopes and expectations. After such an adjustment, if she had been a passenger sailing upon the doomed Titanic, Victoria would have smiled. "At least the water is choppy," she might have remarked, waves closing over her head.

The warrior women, Kitty's traditional foes, had ferociously consented to aiding in the capture of the spiders. Languishing for decades without the exciting adventures, heroic battles, and feats of daring-do as animated by the satisfactorily-savage infant Lily, they were more than ready to exercise rusty skills and even rustier weapons on an actual flesh and blood foe.

Their contribution (like the horse's) was considerable. They had with little hesitation, also been convinced that they alone were capable of guarding the captives, and where better to perform that duty than in their own home, isolated as it was in the abandoned attic? The rough-hewn wooden box was a veritable fortress, since security against the outside world was ever the primitive warriors' first concern. Like the horse, they were enthusiastically diligent about their tasks, and Victoria indeed, needn't have worried.

Emily Bronte need not have worried either, had she been alive to witness the application of her method of dog training upon spiders. This consisted primarily in Kitty strutting boldly up to a defiant arachnid and striking it smartly about the head. Though Emily Bronte might have approved, she could not have anticipated, nor would she have recommended such a strategy, since the instantaneous conclusion of each 'training' session was in the plastic bear being seized by the angry trainee, efficiently bound in silk, and tucked under a bench. Once, twice, thrice; the outcome was the same, for Kitty could not believe a sacrosanct notion held for so many years did not in fact work.

The bear was sipping tea with her dear human friend, and sadly recounting her failures. "If the warrior women had not cut me loose with their swords, I should still be under that bench, quite helpless, and dreading my future. I had so meant that you, dear Victoria, should be spared these failings. I wanted to manage the whole of it myself, only presenting you with the gratifying results."

"But Kitty," Victoria protested, "You were not alone, having been aided by the horse and the warrior women, and I would have been happy to lend my support as well. You need not shoulder this burden alone. Really, it is too much to ask of any single creature. Pray, how many, exactly, spiders have you captured?"

"Just the two. There are others, but they have hidden themselves about the garden and so are not our concern."

Pudding

Having accidentally fallen into a pot of warm pudding Victoria had neglected to put in the fridge, I can state with the strongest authority and the deepest emotion that it is something everyone on earth should try at least once.

Chapter 15

The Mailman Cometh, Again

The woman, who had been companionably strolling about the rooms and hallway of the downstairs of her house chatting with Kitty perched on her shoulder, suddenly stopped, heart in her mouth. Through the glass panels framing the front door she espied a most welcome sight. The delinquent mailman, for it most certainly was he, back after a ten-day absence, stood riveted upon the sidewalk, gazing in slack-jawed amazement at the house. His lips moved soundlessly.

"What...is he...?" Victoria fell silent at the realization the mailman most likely was stricken by the sight of the bloody-red streaks dripping down the front wall.

"What can he be about?" demanded Kitty. "Why should he stand there staring at our house? I shall just slip out and have a word with him..." Victoria managed to prevent this impetuous interesting encounter by efficiently scooping up her friend before she made the attempt.

"Hush, Kitty! Look, he is finally putting my mail in the plastic bag. Hooray! That is all I wanted. That is a triumph in any case." The woman amended, "Perhaps I should have put a notice on the mailbox assuring him the spider is gone. Oh well." She waited, quivering behind the closed door in unapologetic cowardice, before tiptoeing out to recover her mail. On the way out, she recollected that she had nothing of which to fear or be ashamed, for wasn't she a legitimate homeowner going about the legitimate business of common mail retrieval from her own receptacle? With that conviction strengthening her backbone, she casually straightened her shoulders and casually glanced around. To her dismay, the mailman was still loitering about further down the sidewalk, staring fixedly in her direction. With a sheepish, though exaggeratedly casual wave, she snatched the single piece of mail from the bag, darted into the house, and slammed and locked the door.

The mail was a letter from her daughter, the former Butler. "Kitty, look, Lily has written. Perhaps there are pictures of the baby." She bustled off to the kitchen, smiling in anticipation and relief, barely acknowledging the toy bear's smug comment of, "So, she did take my hint!" The two settled themselves companionably at the table; Victoria snug in her favorite hard-wood chair, Kitty propped comfortably atop her friend's bony forearm. The Butler's proud mother read the first line: 'A report of the most alarming nature has reached me...' "What?" she gasped.

Kitty, ever sensitive to Victoria's moods, crowded closer, leaning heavily against the gigantic forearm. "Something amiss, my dear?" She scanned her friend's huge face looming, like a dirigible overhead, centered above the letter. She noted the furrowed brow with its purple swelling, the shocked eyes, the clenched lips. The bear searched her memory for the most likely explanation.

"Something of a disaster, perhaps, with her attempts at cooking dinner? In my opinion, Lily never was quite the cook she professed herself to be. A Butler, however superior, should keep to her station. I hope not to distress you with this opinion..." But Victoria's face remained unresponsive though turning a little pinker, like a dirigible at sunset. "Is it her marriage, then? That patched-up affair? Not the rollicking success she hoped it to be?" Still, no response.

Kitty re-searched through her memory, absentmindedly scratching upon the skin of the human's forearm with overgrown claws. She scanned over a detailed mental examination of the Butler's weaknesses. Astoundingly, there were far and away too many to count. Unresolved old grievances still festered. The stalwart former Butler might have been startled indeed to know that her confederate in all manner of past delightful acts of mayhem, now harbored such notions of resentment and ingratitude. Soon, though, Kitty's interest flagged, as it always did when examining the past, for time is a human concern. Still, as a plastic being, one who had spent more than her share of timelessness locked away inside a suffocating trunk with hostile enemies, time was still a concept pertinent enough to provoke one into losing one's temper.

Victoria flung the letter down upon the table with a snort of outrage. Kitty galloped over in an instant for a sniff, but Victoria had snatched it back up. "I won't have you eating this letter!" she growled. "Really, Kitty, it is too much!"

The bear growled back softly in return. "I must assure you, Dear One, I had no intention of eating your letter from the Butler."

The woman glanced askance at the bear, who was still bristling, this time with indignation. "No, Kitty; no, my dear," she soothed, "of course not. I am referring to...I meant to say...the reports spelled out in this letter are too much. We are being spied upon, if you can believe it, and what is far, far worse, reported on, to Lily the Butler of all people, who lives so far away, and has so many concerns of her own. She should be the last person to be made aware, I mean she should have nothing more to press on her, all our little problems, let alone worry about. I cannot believe..." For one moment her eyes rested on the guileless face of her small toy friend. "No. I will not believe it. Solidarity, you know, after all that we have been through."

The conversation was degenerating into nonsense. Kitty's attention flagged again. So much demands politeness, but further than that! Humans! "If that is all then Victoria, no charming photographs, no domestic disasters, then I must be off. There are spiders needing attention, there are warrior women to relieve of their duties, there are certain 'ideas' I wish to explore."

The human was not listening. Her eyes darted back to the writing on the paper and remained there as the bear 'tch-ed' in disgust and strolled away, un-remarked. "A report of the most alarming nature…" Victoria adjusted her bifocals for maximum penetration and settled down at the kitchen table to analyze the rest of the letter. "Reports of giant spiders; reports of malevolent toys; reports of senile old women wandering the streets muttering; overgrown weeds; blood splashed across the house in a grotesque response to a reasonable request to display a house address in case of emergency; reports of flames and smoke issuing from the vicinity of the backyard during a burn ban." The preposterous list of dangers was alarming indeed.

"No wonder Lily is concerned! This makes it sound appalling. It sounds…well it sounds…it sounds like what happened, actually. Who, but Kitty and myself, was witness to all these events?" The woman stood and walked stiffly to the back door. The scorched place at the bottom of the shed was now concealed by tomato plants; indeed, the plants were fine healthy six-footers heavy with foliage and drooping with green, marble-sized fruit. "When did I plant tomatoes?"

The question died on her tongue as a sound coming from somewhere overhead in the attic of her house drove all conscious thought of earthly matters from her mind. The sound caused a trembling in her knees, and a shiver ran down her thin frame from the very top of her old grey head to the soles of her old grey feet. She remembered that sound, having heard it once before, when she was much younger.

Coffee

Not tea. Don't bother.

Chapter 16
Spiders in the Attic, in Cars

The problem with listening is in not always hearing what is meant to be heard. This sound coming from the attic was unequivocal, and not really a matter of interpretation. But when speaking to Kitty earlier, Victoria had not been listening close enough, or hearing what she should have heard, or she most definitely would have taken alarm at her friend's mention of "other ideas". While she was distracted by her letter, those very same ideas had been put into motion by the intrepid bear with the aid of the warrior women, the reluctant horse, and an assortment of plastic animal friends. Victoria raced to the second floor, slowed her pace across the top hallway, and lingered at the first step of the pull-down ladder leading to the attic. Her heart performed its painful thumping, and her vision cleared as she slumped at the bottom of the steps, just resting, gathering strength. It was when her leaden feet had propelled her head up to the top of the steps and level with the attic floor that the fun began, when a wildly careening heavy metal toy car roared straight toward her face!

She just had time to close her eyes. The expected impact, which she had suffered one time before, long ago, did not happen. After a moment of panicked waiting, she peeked with one watery eye, and saw the car sitting at an angle, inches from her face. Behind the wheel was a very disgruntled-looking spider, gazing ferociously at her from a multitude of shiny red eyes, and waving imperiously with a multitude of hairy legs. "Kitty," Victoria gasped, in quiet desperation, "Kitty, please do come here."

In answer to her prayers, the bear rushed across the attic floor right up to the woman's nose, which was on a level with the bear's feet. The rest of the human, in the manner of a gigantic, animated iceberg, remained out of sight on the steps below. "My dear! You are not hurt?" The bear stroked the human's forehead with her tiny paws, smoothing back an errant curl. "Let me make haste to assure you that though this was not my idea, it was indeed a very bad idea, and I must take full responsibility for it. I should never have allowed that spider so much freedom, at least not so soon. Please assure me you are unhurt, or I shall never forgive myself!"

"Whatever!" the woman murmured faintly, "I mean, whatever is that spider doing in that car?"

Kitty blushed. "Yes, I see you have caught me out in a little white lie; an idea of mine indeed. I've been allowing limited freedoms for good behavior and social participation, but; nature will tell, I'm afraid." The tiny bear hoisted one of Victoria's thin fingers in an effort to assist her friend up the attic steps. When the human obliged, rising so far as to sit comfortably on the attic floor with her legs dangling down and her feet on the steps below in preparation of "a quick getaway", and the spider had been herded by the warrior women back inside their barricaded compound, the bear continued her painful confidence.

"I have found much to admire in these new friends. Did you know they are capable of communicating telepathically?" Victoria admitted she did not, her knowledge of spiders being insufficiently supplied by an indifferent public education. The bear twirled madly all around while she continued to speak. The woman supposed her to be trying out some celebratory form of dance steps, when upon closer examination, she discovered the true cause of the gyrations to be simply an effort at untangling the myriad strands of lint and feather-stuck spider web bedecking her person. When these were successfully dislodged, Kitty made one last brush at the remnants of her apron and resumed.

"I have learned one must not display weakness of any sort. A spider will strike when within range upon the slightest sign of trembling. It rouses something quite primitive and intentionally frightening." She leaned in closer. "I must admit my opinion of the virtues and bravery of our friends the warrior women has been shaken. Though suffering just cause to be frightened, perhaps you noticed them displaying the most un-warrior-like grimaces of horror, as they dashed away to safety?"

The human looked keenly about and espied the warriors crouching miserably behind their compound. The skeptical glances they shot her way convinced her their nerves had been severely tried. "But, Kitty, they have always performed their role in whatever you have asked of them and have done so in this instance admirably. Everyone has a breaking point, as I have cause to know. One mustn't shove, must one?"

"I suppose you are right. The warriors were quite indomitable until the spiders were let out of their compound and became so mobile. Spiders love speed, if you can believe it, and are heedlessly reckless drivers. They have been crashing about in this car with abandon." The bear leaned in to whisper, "I believe they were hoping to run over the warriors, thus incapacitating them, in order to make a meal of them! I would have enjoyed seeing that battle! Fierce warriors indeed! Without a foe, we are all fierce warriors, aren't we?"

"Kitty, you haven't!" Victoria glanced with pity towards the cowering plastic toys, still in hiding. "Well, no wonder. Between the shrill cries of the warriors and the sounds of that car crashing into the walls, I thought we were reliving the days of Miss Hruchkukk! My nerves are quite shattered, Kitty, I assure you. Much more of this I cannot stand."

"Tut tut. You must not give way and indulge your human propensity for exaggeration when we are so close to finding an elegant solution to this vexing problem. The spiders have been proving amenable to my training techniques..." Here Kitty had the grace to turn her face aside, hiding her expression, for

Victoria was only too well aware that the Emily Bronte method had unforeseen drawbacks. "Though the spiders have eagerly agreed to and have honestly attempted to submit to my training methods," she corrected, anticipating Victoria's reaction, "they will fall victim to their own natures. They continually forget themselves in their anxiety to procure an easy meal. In this I fear they are much mistaken in thinking I myself am such a target. I believe one of them has permanently damaged a fang trying to pierce my neck, if you can believe it!"

Victoria expressed her deep concern at this and drew Kitty into her lap to assess the damage to the bear's neck. There she found, most shockingly, not just one single puncture wound having gone completely through the plastic neck, but several shallower stabs leaving visible dents.

"This must stop at once, my dear. It is quite shocking! I can no longer countenance your efforts at taming these monsters, for monsters they have proven to be. I myself do not believe they are tamable in the least. And, if memory serves, I do not recall spiders ever belonging to the ARA." This last was a low blow at the sworn representative of that league of militant wild animals, which in typical fashion the bear failed to register. "Please do tell me you share my opinion! Somehow, we will together clear them from the house. We have done something similar before. If you will remember the ordeal with Miss Hruchkukk?"

Victoria had been expecting an argument. Her friend, once embarked upon a course of action, was not readily dissuaded. She had not abandoned her attempt at living naturally in the woods, "Thoreauing it", until stymied by an unusual and devastating series of natural disasters. And she had not been capable of self-control in the matter of taking over Victoria's kitchen to cook a meal until she had demolished the entire house. So, it was with surprise, the human heard the bear sigh hugely, and admit, "You are right. You are quite right."

"I'd rather expected an argument, you know, Miss Kitty. Perhaps...perhaps you are feeling your age?"

"My age is as much the same as yours as makes no never-mind, though I do not show it as you do. I do not argue the point because I must agree with it. You are right and this endeavor has been a failure. I am convinced Emily Bronte herself would have retreated after that first savage bite."

Butter

Everything is better with butter. Everything.

Chapter 17
Postal Requirements for Mailing Livestock

In the end, it had been incumbent upon Victoria to see the spiders completely and satisfactorily removed from the vicinity. The warrior women, having stood for just about all they were willing to stand, were united in a remarkably successful peaceful protest. Considering their usual methods of displaying disapproval, involving sharpened spears, blood-curdling cries, and prolonged sieges, it was perplexing to find the warriors now simply pretending to be inanimate, comatose, plastic dolls. This method involved them lying rigidly propped against the back wall of their house, starring glassily at nothing and failing to respond when pressed for participation. The human took compassion upon the small toys, for she, better than most, understood that they were subject to stresses well beyond the call of duty. After all they were not even Kitty's particular friends or her own, merely unallied acquaintances at best.

The woman could not budge their house loose from the attic floor. Long dusty years of being rooted in one spot had welded the heavy wooden box firmly into place, and so, unable to move the mountain, she resorted to moving the mote in its eye by capturing those eight-legged fiends in a plastic butter dish with a tight-fitting lid. Her heart thumped erratically, and she was drenched in sweat before the huge spiders were persuaded to be locked up in this new prison.

"I was so afraid they should lunge at me," she confided to the casually on-looking Miss Kitty. Aside from providing an insipid cheer or two, that animal had proven useless in persuading the arachnids to vacate what they now plainly considered their own comfortable new territory. Indeed, there was scarcely a square inch of the interior of the warriors' compound that was devoid of thick drapings of web. Flies, gnats, mosquitoes, millipedes, silverfish, and other assorted insects were gone there to their doom within the shimmering veils.

The human discreetly avoided taking any notice of the flurry of activity now coming from the warriors' reclaimed abode, as well as the frightful language, violent thrashings, and black clouds of dust and debris floating onto the attic floor. "I suppose they feel justified, Kitty, in dumping this upon our heads." She tried for sympathy but was only able to attain a thin version of it.

Kitty peered searchingly through the accumulating piles of rubble, making an accounting of her findings. "Twenty, twenty-five, thirty, desiccated corpses if I'm not mistaken, Victoria." She tapped a fang thoughtfully with a blunted claw. "You may want to reconsider removing these spiders, hasty one. Your attic is disgustingly full of bugs! How was I ever persuaded to live up here for so many years?"

"Well, what do you propose as the alternative? I thought we were both of the opinion that it is best to remove these spiders far a 'field, and I am in the process of doing so, you know. It has been my intention, as it unsettles me greatly to know there are such creatures…"

The bear waved a paw, dismissing human intentions. "I must assure you that I too have had my fill of them. Ungrateful, irrational creatures! I shall not miss them one little bit. Permanent holes in my hide, Victoria! However, there is the matter of their obvious usefulness. Cannot you leave them as they were, imprisoned quite handily inside the warrior's house so that they may continue their function of removing the bugs from your attic? All of nature strives to fulfill its function…"

Here the bear was drowned out by a storm of outrage. The warriors, roused to action at last, presenting a united front, were stung into defense of their home. They surged from the house, fully intending some sort of mayhem, menacing the woman and their toy bear arch-enemy with fearsome cries and upraised weapons.

Victoria had scooped up the bear, thrusting her atop her shoulder and well out of reach. Since Kitty's removal from the attic these many years, and the warriors' reinstatement back into that roomy isolated floor of the house which they had occupied all by themselves for so long, so satisfactorily, the tiny fierce women felt more than justified in raising the roof.

Without the daily trial of 'Running Mouth' and her assorted annoying small animal friends, these primitives had settled into a comfortable routine much to their liking. Though Victoria often thought with pity of them overhead in that cold dark place, they required none, since never had they been happier. Even during that odd period when unaccountably playing a major role in driving Victoria out of her mind for her own good, their participation had not been one to induce gaiety since they had been called up for duty in pieces: arms and legs, and Tuk-Thuk's severed head. And even being animated by that inconsiderate Butler in the distant past, there had been misery and discontent, for she had shown little understanding of, or interest in the simplest of their tribal rituals, customs, or lives.

Victoria had instinctively drawn away, avoiding the prodding of sharpened spears, but Kitty was made of sterner stuff. She sprang down Victoria's shirt front, gripped her belt like the rope on a pirate ship and swung to the floor to confront them, an act of true bravery since not only was she a full two inches shorter than her traditional adversaries, she was unequivocally deeply hated by them. "No. No, my dears!" she shouted, "That will not happen. Your house shall belong only to you. That others will occupy it is out of the question. Please do calm yourselves." Out of the side of her mouth, she stage-whispered, "I have spoken to the human on your behalf, and I will not allow you to be incommoded any longer."

Thanks to Victoria's restorative efforts years ago, the warriors' arms and legs were now very securely attached to their bodies with stainless steel tie-wire, making them so much more vigorous and robust than when bought new from the toy factory. They were also expert markswomen, as the human had cause to remember.

"Ow! Ouch!" Kitty cried "That was uncalled for! Please stop the rampaging at once. Your home has been restored to you all and shall not be taken away again! I have given my solemn promise!" Victoria had made herself useful, hastily grabbing a broom and sweeping away the majority of the cobwebs from the interior of the warriors' home even as Kitty spoke. "There, you see? As she was instructed, Victoria has made everything as good as new."

With a parting jab of her spear as she passed, Tuk-Thuk, the brawniest and least civilized of the quartet, stalked with her sisters into the house and dropped the rolled leather door into place. There were two very audible snaps, as the wooden rod holding the leather was secured into place by the heavy metal clamps on the floor. Kitty, skirts a 'tumble, pulled herself onto Victoria's knee.

"I have made things right with them, Victoria dear," she whispered somewhat breathlessly, "though I believe for some reason they insist on blaming you for all the hubbub. Let us retire to a place of neutrality before they become unsettled once more." She nimbly climbed up Victoria's shirt, and leapt athletically into her pocket, meanly jeering in the direction of the warriors, "And don't bother yourselves to see us off!"

When the bear and her human friend were retired to the safety of the bedroom floor below, with the spiders still enclosed in their butter dish on the dresser, a general sigh of exasperation went out. "Kitty, I cannot imagine what I am to do now. If I take these spiders out as far as I can in the garden, will I have their assurance they will remain there? Can I trust them to do what is right? In effect, I am questioning their natural ethical code. I don't know for certain if spiders practice an ethical code of behavior, do you? I know only with conviction that I cannot risk their returning to the house; indeed I shall not sleep from this time forward for fear of them crawling over my face in the night." She glanced at the butter dish-prison, which was being rocked erratically from within as the spiders vented their frustration. The human set a heavy lamp on top of the dish, shuddering as she did so. "Nightmare!"

Piteously, the bear clasped her paws under her chin. "And yet we must do something quickly before the air in that container runs out. They might even now be suffocating!" She turned a distressed face towards her friend, expecting to meet with a confirming grimace of horror mirroring her own. Indeed, a show of fellow feeling was what was to be expected. Instead, the bear was shocked into silence.

A horrid idea was seen to be flickering across Victoria's face like the spasm of a candle-flame before it is blown out. The human's eyes revealed that a thought dwelt in her brain for just a second, a thought so unlike her, so horribly horrid; but so fleeting. Kitty was almost unsure she had witnessed the struggle over temptation there. And yet she was quite sure.

"You are right," Victoria said. "While we consider what best to do, let us take the spiders out to the garden." Kitty was remarkably silent. She struggled mightily with her own temptation, but wisely allowed it to evaporate without acting on it. Indeed Victoria had done the same, and isn't the deliberate mutual ignorance of our friends' weaknesses the very essence of friendship?

There was a strong steel-wire cage on the patio, two feet long, one foot wide, and one foot high, wrapped in window screening, and designed as a humane trap for other unwelcome wild creatures, into which Victoria dumped the reluctant arachnids. Made torporous by their time in the hot and airless butter dish, they moved but sluggishly, wondering no doubt, what they had gotten themselves into now. In the manner of spiders, they lived only in the present and so were unable to imagine the true precariousness of their position.

There was no question about it. Victoria had long since passed being able to hike any distance into the surrounding forest and extensive fields beyond her garden walls, with the assurance she should be able to return within a reasonable time before nightfall, if at all. "I am not a spring chicken," she murmured, "or a goat or dancing bear. I cannot take these creatures far enough away for my own reassurance, especially under my own power, unless I send them off in the mail."

A small scream erupted from her throat! An answering scream echoed back from Kitty. "Why not? Why not?" she demanded. "A perfect solution to all our problems!"

The friends giggled with relief. They held their sides in identical positions of repressed hilarity. "What do we need to do first?" they asked each other. "We need to supply them with an ample amount of juicy and palatable insects, so they do not hunger or thirst. A piece of apple, one of banana, and a small chunk of raw hamburger left in one corner of the cage should do it. We must enlarge a few holes in the wire mesh to allow the free passage of their meals. Stout brown wrapping paper with holes left strategically just so, and..."

"To whom should we mail it?" This question propelled both the human and the toy bear into unladylike uncontrolled fits of merriment. Simultaneously, the answer dawned on both: "Lily, the Butler!" they shouted, tears of joy racing down their cheeks. "She will love getting mail!"

Old Stuff

Do not under any circumstance listen to a human when the question of the edibility of food comes up. Humans are picky eaters who refuse perfectly delicious foodstuff if it seems at all on the elderly side. Just when the bouquet is ripest, the flavors aged to perfection, the texture ideal for slurping, humans will throw out, for instance, a most delectable fruit, or lasagna, or bowl of salad. Utter insanity!

Chapter 18

The Solution to Spiders, At Last

The idea of her daughter and baby grandson opening an international package containing two huge and possibly lethal spiders soon quelled the human's glee and sobered her back into a frame of right-thinking.

Miss Kitty's thoughts were a good deal more personal and characteristic of a very small being. The possibility of sending two spiders on such a long journey into the unknown, a journey she herself had once been forced to undertake to the doll hospital when in need of re-flocking, extinguished all levity and caused a wrinkle to furrow the bear's forehead.

"For we should not be happy, you know, if they were to die." Not wanting to seem unfeeling towards the other life forms with whom she shared the planet, or weak, Victoria conveniently remembered that there were possible federal restrictions on sending livestock through the postal service, punishable by huge fines.

While the two were considering what next to do, Kitty wandered over to the cage, a roomy prison now quite shrouded with dense webs. The enticing pieces of fruit in the corners were invisible beneath them. She suddenly exclaimed, "My dear, I believe our problem may have solved itself for us! Pray, do look here!"

Victoria dropped painfully down to her arthritic knees to peer into the cage resting on the flagstones outside the back door. "What is it Kitty?" The bear shushed her. "Just watch."

There came a flicker, then a vibration, then a shudder, and quick as thought, an unlucky small thing perished in the jaws of the caged spiders. "OOH," the watchers exclaimed involuntarily. They retreated to the living room where they sat staring forlornly into each other's eyes.

"It is nature, Kitty, to eat and be eaten. All living things do it. We must not be squeamish now, must we?"

"I am hardly 'squeamish' Victoria! I am, if anything, filled with admiration at the efficiency of the hunting. Did not you see the lack of cruelty or hesitation? Just a swift and merciful execution. And now, I wonder, may we not safely return these caged creatures to the attic? They are confined. There is no affront to the warriors, or potential danger to Lily and her offspring. The spiders will live full and satisfying lives most agreeably while performing a necessary function for others. Isn't that the best that life can offer?"

And so, the strange journey of two unrelated arachnids led them from Victoria's backyard shed and her front-yard mailbox through a course of events both terrifying, life-threatening, and perplexing, including: a trial by fire, the Emily Bronte method of dog training, misguided application of the Emily Post guide to manners and domestication; to an unusually satisfying conclusion within the safe confines of a cage in an attic of a human house, protected from all storms and enemies, and mystifyingly provided with sustenance, and with scrupulous attention to detail for the remainder of their two-month life-spans.

Toast and Butter

There can be nothing finer or more inclined to satisfy both the nutritional as well as the aesthetic requirements of a person of the usual degree of intelligence than hot crispy toasted bread slathered in salty butter. Butter should drip from the bread. If no bread is at hand, then butter may be licked straight from the dish if no one is watching.

Chapter 19

A Mailman in The House

"Ahem, and pardon!"

The male voice, coming as it did behind an unsuspecting Victoria's back through an opened kitchen window, sent her from the lip-smacking enjoyment of a deliciously illegal breakfast of ham and eggs with plenty of hot buttered toast, into a near-cardiac event. She sprang from her chair with violence, spinning it crashing to the floor, while darting horrified glances at the shadowy figure peering in at her. Dazzling early morning sunlight backlit his face, obscuring it.

Her heart calmed, breathing slowed, pulse was restored to near normal rate, when inexplicably, the elderly woman recognized her interlocutor. "Oh," she quavered, "The Mailman. You startled me."

The Mailman, for it was he indeed who had been standing stiffly, almost as if at attention, bowed deeply and profoundly from the waist. His genuflection was so severe and long-lasting, Victoria was encouraged to move timorously closer to the window to peer out, in case he should require assistance, having become stuck staring at his own feet. When he sprang suddenly erect, she was taken aback, and fumbled feeble fingers at her chin and hair.

"My apologies, Madam. If you will be so kind; I find I am compelled to ask a question requiring an immediate answer." He waited, eyeing her intently, until she managed a grave nod. "If I may; am I to continue the delivery of your mail to the torn plastic bag hanging from the mailbox? If you will not take offense and will accept advice from someone in an official postal capacity, I must urge caution against it. You may not wish to entrust your vital bits of information there."

Though he spoke so strangely and formally, the Mailman's words were to the point. Victoria's preoccupation with the spiders living in her attic had prevented her from seeing to other, more mundane routines. She had not been to check the mail for some time. Important and vital bits might indeed even now be blowing hither and yon about her front gate.

"Oh, Oh yes. I see what you mean. Thank you. I will go see to it. Right now."

"Shall I meet you at the gate then?" Her startled expression caused the man to pause. "I mean, if you wish, I shall join you at the gate. Then. Shall I?"

"Yes, yes, all right then. As soon as I can. Let me...I must first find my shoes and jacket." The old woman was speechless with embarrassment at the oddity of it all. That someone should have intruded upon her sanctuary, passing the gated and walled perimeter up to her very kitchen window, was less a concern than the humiliation of being caught eating voluminous quantities of butter, and in her bare feet! She donned her ratty house slippers and a light jacket, took a deep calming breath, gravely opened the front door, and saw that she was awaited. Sharply drawing in a series of those shallow staccato breaths of oxygen which are rumored to be so calming, she joined the expectant civil servant at the gate.

To say that the plastic bag was torn was an understatement. It had been ripped to tatters. Victoria combed her fingers through the shreds of plastic, looking questioningly at the man who had exited the garden, closing the gate firmly behind him, and was now standing opposite her on the other side of the fence.

"You must comprehend that I could not in good conscience continue to deliver your mail. You must comprehend that I felt my function at this time to be less mail delivery, than mail futility; for anything deposited in that ghost of a bag should be less delivered than dematerialized."

He stood, straight as a ramrod, smiling faintly and fixing his gaze somewhere on a point in the distance beyond her head. He waited. The woman blinked. "I feel as if I'm in a novel. Am I in a trance?"

"If you will permit? That response is not compatible with this particular situation."

Victoria shook the fog from her brain. "Why didn't you just put the mail in the mailbox? That spider has been gone for some time. You see?" She tugged on the stiff door, finally opening it to display the empty box.

The Mailman stooped to stare inside the mailbox. He stammered in embarrassment. "My deepest apologies, Madam. I seem to have overlooked the obvious, to my chagrin. There indeed is proof of the absence of the problem. Pray, do forgive me."

Not being able to control herself any longer, Victoria blurted out, "Why on earth do you talk like that?"

The Mailman drew himself upright, sucking in a sharp breath. "Again, my apologies. Do forgive my forwardness. I supposed, you see, that we were on the same page, acting quite within the boundaries of our tentative new roles." He paused, uncertain of saying more, but judging something more was required upon observing Victoria's continuing befuddled expression. He leaned in confidentially. "I may have been mistaken. The Butler, you see, has offered me the job. I have consented to accept it. With your approval, of course." He straightened, beaming with the happy expectation of assurance.

Though almost speechless with astonishment, Victoria was no stranger to the niceties of social protocol and the demands of formal civility. "Your name, sir. I demand to know your name."

Once more, the Mailman bowed deeply from the waist, remaining bent in two. "Hoggbend," he proclaimed in the direction of her feet. He sprang erect, his face slightly pink. "Both singular and astonishing, so I've been told. Nonetheless, Hoggbend it is, Ma'am. A family name of long and illustrious lineage. At your service."

Overcome, and without another word, Victoria snatched the small bundle of mail held between his rigid fingers, and turning sharply on her ancient bedroom slippers, marched back the walk, up the steps, through the front door and slammed it shut behind her!

"Kitty! Miss Katherine!" she roared, on her way to the kitchen, "Please do answer me at once!"

Kitty, who was already in the kitchen atop the massive old wooden table, had been lapping Victoria's abandoned cup of heavily-sugared, overly-creamed tea, now cooled to just the right lukewarm temperature. She raised questioning eyes to her friend without ceasing her engrossing activity. One must seize the moment when one can. The bear observed that her human friend trembled. Her hands were shaking, her eyes swam with tears, her voice crackled with outrage. It all seemed a bit melodramatic.

"It is just a cup of tea, my dear," she remarked soothingly. "You shall soon make another. Besides, this one had gone cold, which I know you dislike."

Victoria sank down into her chair. With a visible effort, she composed herself. "It is not the tea. Even though you have not been invited. I fully comprehend..." Of a sudden, as if a gate had opened, a garden gate, the flood burst out. "Oh, what is the difference? I have been betrayed!" she wailed, "And by my own daughter!"

Kitty had just succeeded in quieting her huge friend, not omitting an opportunity to snatch several large bites of ham from her plate, when there came a decided rap upon the kitchen door.

"OOOH!" they screamed in unison. The dark figure looming outside the open window was nothing more than a shadow against the brilliant rays of sunshine. "I know who it is, Kitty," Victoria faintly whispered. "It is that pestilential Mailman. He is the cause of all my distress... what are you doing?"

Kitty, all unbeknownst to her friend, had slid down the rungs of the chair to the floor, and was pulling on the thin chain connected to a pulley, a device which allowed a four inch tall toy bear to open an eight foot door without assistance. Victoria had rigged up the device some years back for Kitty's convenience as well as her own. Now she was filled with a bitter regret for that thoughtfulness. The deed was done. The door swung wide, and upon Kitty's eager invitation, the Mailman stepped smartly across the threshold, right into the elderly woman's home.

Spray Cheese

OH! How long have I suffered when there is such a thing as cheese in a can! One can direct a delightful stream right into one's mouth. How delightful. And satisfactory!

Chapter 20

A Proper Butler, at Long Last

"Just right," Victoria beamed. "You have captured the essence perfectly." The aroma of freshly brewed tea; the water collected during a thunderstorm, filtered through pink and white magnolia blossoms, brought to a gentle boil in an enameled, heavy kettle; the tea leaves plucked by hand from the very tips of the plants, dried on open-weave screens in the hot sunshine; lightly fermented and blended for robust yet genteel flavor; steeped for precisely five minutes, decanted into a porcelain teapot and poured into fine translucent China cups, was perfection unmatched in modern history. One almost hated to add sugar and cream to such a masterpiece, but Kitty was a stickler for convention. Victoria sipped her tea, and since she knew how much it was awaited and breathlessly expected, sighed blissfully. The Butler, hovering at her elbow, permitted himself a faint smile, and modestly withdrew.

Victoria sipped again, and then again. She set her half-empty cup back into its saucer with an audible clink. She stared pensively out the window. "I must just have a word," she thought sternly. "It's—well, it's so silly. The Butler needn't stay bowed down so far from the waist, and backing out, when withdrawing! It smacks of pretension. But, how to word it without insulting him. He is as prickly about the perceived demands of his profession as Kitty is about her size." She did not mention aloud her private objections to that four inch tall toy bear, who remained blissfully unaware of anything amiss. She, at least, having become spoiled by the perfect service, now demanded nothing less.

The Butler, the second to serve in that household, was named Hoggbend. So Victoria had been informed, though she could manage to believe it only with concentrated effort. Mr. Ernie Hoggbend, who had come to her upon the recommendation of her daughter, the original Butler.

"She and I are former schoolmates, you see. Modome may not remember, I do not flatter myself, that I have had the rare good fortune, Modome, to have enjoyed a tea party or two, as guest, within these very same walls, as a lad."

He raised a perfectly round, sugar-crystalled cookie between silver tongs in his immaculately-white-gloved hand, holding it to the light. "I have had the privilege, Modome, of eating cookies from this very recipe at this very same table, oh, so long ago."

"And now, Hoggbend, you are enjoying the privilege of making them for us!" was Kitty's pragmatic observation. "Take care there is not an excess of breakage."

"Certainly, Modome! The absence of a thing, in this case: crumbs, is a Quixotic nullity I shall fully enjoy producing; this shall be my top priority. I am happy to report that I am considered exceedingly careful in this, as in all aspects of improbable though scientifically possible acts of domestic service."

Victoria hastened to reassure the mailman-turned-butler that there was no doubt in her mind as to the truthfulness of his statement. "Satisfactory, Hoggbend. Most satisfactory indeed."

So, as Victoria watched the Butler exiting the room, bowed over from the waist, backing out so that the top of his balding head was the last of him to be seen, she felt she needed to speak. The weight of the conviction pressed upon her conscience. She had observed that it was only with some difficulty that he was able to maneuver into a position conducive to being able to pull the kitchen door shut behind him. Perhaps that was the point on which she might make her correction. Safety, and surely a doubled-up Butler could not be held to the Standards of Domestic Practice Act. Where on earth had he gotten his training?

Victoria released her pent-up suspense in a great sigh, turned to her friend, and hissed, "Kitty! We must take care! There is something irksome...that is to say, I do not wish to ruffle Hoggbend's feelings. Where on earth shall we ever find another such as him?"

That bear winced. "There is no need for such delicacy, Victoria! You may cease your irritating whispering and freely speak your mind." Under her breath, but quite audibly, she muttered, "Hissing at me! What am I now, a goose?"

As usual, Victoria preferred not to hear what she did not want to hear. "But I fear to hurt the Butler's feeling by being too blunt with even this very slight objection. However shall I do it? How to word a slight correction? Do help me."

"Say nothing is my advice, on this as on every other occasion. However, you may speak freely if it is truly what you desire to do. I must mention that you shall not hurt anyone's feelings because a true Butler, one of his caliber, has no feelings to speak of. His vocation requires a complete absence of emotion. Also, unless I have mistaken his regular schedule, he himself has achieved complete absence of being, since is gone."

Victoria was startled. "Gone?"

"Yes, gone upon his rounds. Inconvenient, I call it, since I have just discovered I cannot comfortably reach that plate of delectable pastries he's managed to secrete so cleverly on top of the refrigerator!" She glanced obliquely at her giant friend. "I don't suppose..."

Victoria was distracted. "Oh, he has gone then? I did not think...but then of course, Hoggbend is not our exclusive property, but is also a servant of the government. Quite commendable that he should be able to attend to our needs as well to the needs of all our neighbors. In his official capacity."

Somehow it rang hollow. After a brief pause, "Commendable. We must be generous then, in word as well as in deed, mustn't we?"

"Especially when there is no alternative."

"As you say, when there is no alternative."

Kitty was engrossed by her efforts to gain the platter of delicacies left so inconsiderately beyond her reach. She had just discovered a very large rubber band and was even now attempting to slingshot herself through the air in quest of those tantalizing morsels. Unfortunately, or fortunately, depending upon how one is feeling at the moment about the small plastic toy bear, Victoria noticed in time, and without ceremony, snatched her friend from the jaws of certain doom before the solo flight was attempted.

"Stop that," she commanded automatically. "Please... whatever are you about anyway?"

"That platter of good things left quite beyond my ability to...examine them," began Kitty with a note of rising exasperation. "An examination to ascertain if they are still wholesome and fresh. Really, Victoria, you continue to overlook essentials in your pursuit of inconsequentials. Of what use is it to either of us if the Butler enjoys an existence beyond our doors, if he does not attend to his duties within our doors? It is like a tree falling in the woods with no one to hear it. Squirrels do not count. How am I to eat...I mean examine, those temptations if they are left beyond my reach?"

This entire exchange was baffling. Victoria stared empty-headed at her friend, until her eyes were directed upward by the pointing of Kitty's paw. "I must point out the obvious once more, I'm afraid, Kitty my dear, that your appetite far outweighs your judgment, on this as on many other occasions. I wish you would take your behavior in hand before disaster, always looming, overtakes us both."

"In paw, dear one, in paw. Otherwise a pretty speech, fine sentiment."

Strange as it was to have an unexpected Butler appear within her house without warning, it was stranger still at the rapidity with which he had become an intrinsic part of the household. Indeed, he had made himself all but indispensable. The elderly woman shook her head at the wonder of it all. And there was the matter of his unquestioning acceptance of the tiny plastic toy bear too! The Butler not only spoke to and responded in an unaffected manner to the four inch high Miss Kitty, clearly showing his awareness of her and his sanctioning of this unusual phenomenon, but also seeming completely comfortable doing so.

Victoria was perplexed by this for some time until realizing that her daughter, the former Butler, must have given this, her replacement, a thorough vetting before releasing him upon her mother. His ability to see and speak with a toy bear, though magical, was therefore understandable, for he should not have been able to make such astonishing inroads to the household if he had not already been in possession of an unusual imagination as well as acute perception, which up till now, had been found lacking in everyone else outside of their private family circle.

"Of course Lily has known him this long while, so he says, from childhood. I can't imagine she should have permitted him to darken my door if he had not been able to perceive Kitty's importance in our lives." The woman sighed. "I have admitted to the unusualness of my relationship with Kitty. It was never an issue with Lily, since she shared in it. Indeed, now that I think back on it, it was she who first introduced Kitty to me. Yes! All those notes tossed at me from behind doors and out of windows! I remember screaming most shamefully the first time I realized Kitty was a living being. With her child's imagination, Lily brought her toy bear to life, animating her with exquisite detail till she has become as real to me as any other friend, and then more so. I doubt with the passing of the years and Lily's metamorphosis into adulthood, that she is now able to speak with Kitty as she once did. But it is not she, rather the outside world that has always been our problem."

Once more she enjoyed the calm satisfaction, of feeling safe and happy and complete inside her own home. Then, as so often occurs in those who have lived long enough to understand the true state of affairs, weathering all the ups and downs that more often than not are simply long dragged-out downs with mere whiffs of ups, a disquieting thought sprang up. "I can't believe it, but I do suspect that this Hoggbend person must be the source of all the spying that's been going on, and the reporting! Lily could not have been aware of the events occurring inside my house otherwise."

At once her peace was shattered. "What a double-edged sword! He has gained my confidence, and insinuated himself into my life almost unquestioned, in order that he might keep tabs on me for the absent Lily. I do not know if I am more offended or saddened."

A tap on the door was followed by its opening and the polite coughing of that Butler himself. "Modome, your tea is ready. Shall I serve it in here?"

"Yes," she answered absently. "But...well...I could have sworn; didn't I just have tea not more than a few minutes ago?"

The Butler appeared taken aback. "Indeed, not. How very fortunate! it must be that Modome has achieved that place in her life where time does seem to pass by so quickly. Almost in the blink of an eye. The Golden Years." He placed down a tray brimming with delicious-looking items as well as a steaming pot of tea, and then hesitantly, "Shall I invite Miss Kitty to join you as usual? I believe her to be napping."

"As you please." The human sighed. Déjà vu all over again. She decided to speak, not caring the cost. "I was under the impression...I mean, weren't you supposed to be off on your rounds, Hoggbend? Your postal route? Kitty led me to believe it was your time to go round the neighborhood delivering mail. I should hate for you to neglect your other duties."

His face twisted in astonishment. What a very small mouth he had! His bushy black eyebrows raised up in comical inverted U's, his tiny mouth making an 'O', and his chin all but invisible! A vivid red scar Victoria had not noticed before ran from his mouth to the corner of his left eye. Really! The Butler was an astonishing-looking person. However it had happened, that he and Victoria's daughter should have become friends, was another thing that needed answering, for the old woman could not remember such a childhood visitor. And yet, he claimed to have attended their private tea parties!

"That was indeed the case, Modome, though some time past, hours in fact. Thank you, for your concern. My usual rounds were completed yesterday in the usual time, whereas today's were somewhat abbreviated." He coughed discreetly behind his gloved hand. "Miss Kitty, if I may be so bold, has been suggesting improvements. She let slip the hint that at this particular time there might be an increased need for my services, here. Therefore I have endeavored to accelerate the completion of my appointed rounds by the judicious sorting and disposal of unnecessary items, that I may be of better use. Here." He beamed, awaiting her approval.

Far from offering the expected gracious 'Thank you', Victoria was speechless with dismay. "Do you...pray, are you...the unnecessary items...you are referring to junk mail, aren't you? Circulars?" To hide her confusion, she nervously twisted her fingers in her tangled grey hair.

"Please, Modome, if you will permit me?" The Butler whipped a silver comb from some hidden pocket and proceeded to untangle Victoria's hair to her great astonishment. "Modome has hit the nail on the head! Junk mail it is!" At her continued silence, he prattled on. "I must admit to a certain fondness for this task, for you see, if I am not presuming too much by revealing aspects of my own personal history? I trained as a hairdresser for some time, before my acceptance into the civil service, and had enjoyed the privilege of styling my own mother's hair for her, before her passing."

This astounding revelation was not of an order for which Victoria was able to intelligently respond. "Oh," she muttered feebly. "How nice. Not her passing, of course! But your caring for her."

"Thank you for your kind indulgence, dear Modome." He carefully lifted the thinning hair away from the left side of her forehead. "I have observed, if you please, this very large, discolored lump just here. May I ask if it is the cause of pain?"

Victoria raised a shaking hand to the spot and encountered the huge, solid swelling. "After all this time! I'd quite forgotten it! Well, I guess it wasn't all that long ago, or maybe it was. Why yes, that happened when that dead branch stabbed me. It shot through the air, Hoggbend, with such precision and velocity, almost as if my forehead was its intended target! A bullseye! One is apt to forget that trees are living beings, and may harbor grievances, although I cannot recall ever having done anything to offend that particular...Oh! Well, perhaps my snapping off that branch, even though it was quite dead, must have been most provoking! I do see that now."

The Butler retained an impassive countenance. "Quite. Is the wound a source of pain?"

"Hardly at all. I had quite forgot it." She gently rubbed the surprisingly large and still tender lump.

"Very good, Modome. If you are quite finished with your tea, I shall remove these articles." With a theatrical flourish of his soft white cloth over the table top, the Butler picked up the tea tray and withdrew. He had devised a new method for the bent-over exiting of a room with heavy tray in hand, a complicated maneuver involving unseen fingertip fumblings and twiddlings behind his back, and so accomplished his self-removal with a degree of grace and efficiency.

Victoria sat for a while in silence. 'Has Kitty then spoken to him? He still withdraws bent over, but he's so much more refined about it.' She thought a little more. 'Come to think of it, to where exactly, does that man withdraw? I mean, this is my home, isn't it? I certainly have never had a Butler's pantry.' She rose from her chair as soundlessly as possible and tiptoed across to the swinging kitchen door. A furtive peep without disclosed no signs of the Butler lurking in the hall, and so she made bold to sneak cautiously, heart pounding, throughout the ground-floor rooms of her own house, searching for him. "I'll bet Kitty knows of his whereabouts!" With that happy thought, she slunk into the living-room calling softly, "Kitty! Kitty. I require your assistance. At once!"

To her consternation, the bear was not to be found. Kitty's Barton Cottage stood quite empty.

Churning Butter

If in dire straits, such as when the powers that be refuse one a required daily allowance of butter, here is a simple way to make it: attach a small jar filled with heavy cream and tightly lidded, to the nearest large human's pant cuff with a string tightly knotted. The humans will not notice at all, and the movement of their huge legs will churn a satisfactory glob of butter in no time.

Chapter 21

When a Mailman Oversteps

The elderly woman woke with a snort and a start. "What the...?" She sat bolt upright on the couch where she had, apparently, been napping. "I don't even remember lying down. Good gracious, is that 7:00 a.m. or 7:00 p.m.?" By the intensity of the light flooding the living room through the glass panes of the patio doors, it appeared to be morning. "I slept all night on the couch?" She coughed.

She was too stricken with the indignity of it all; an elderly woman passed out overnight upon her own sofa in her own living room...heavens! What in the world might people think? She coughed again as a harsh smell tickled her nose. "What the...?" She struggled to her feet, now coughing repeatedly.

Flickering shadows drew her out to the kitchen and the window overlooking the garden. Flames danced up to the rooftop. With a shriek of horror, the old woman plunged into the yard, found the garden hose, and with fumbling fingers, directed a forceful spray of icy water onto the tongues of fire. An answering shriek made her doubt her senses; had she been shrieking without knowing it? The high-pitched sound screeched on and on, long after she'd shut off the water.

The sound tapered off. The flames were vanquished, and except for a tell-tale ribbon of black smoke rising up from the sodden ashes, all was serene. Except for the tiny figure of Miss Kitty, rolling on the ground clutching her sides laughing in hysterics, and the erect wrathful figure of Hoggbend gazing at Victoria in stony disbelief as water dripped from his nose and chin, and sluiced in rivulets down his Proper Butler's black attire, and puddled in his shoes.

"Heh," he cleared his throat.

A panting Miss Kitty squeaked breathlessly, "I told you so! I told you so!"

Hoggbend closed his eyes. "My mistake. Modome. Please, do excuse me while I...I freshen up." He squelched off into the house, wringing water from his coat tails and sleeves as he went. Behind him, barely visible through the diminishing though thick black smoke were the skeletal outlines of the garden shed.

"Kitty," Victoria hissed, "What is the meaning of this?"

"Oh, my dear! You will scarce believe me, but that Butler was burning down the garden shed!"

Victoria stood thunderstruck. "Why on earth? Why should he have thought of doing such a thing?" she demanded. "There is no earthly reason for a Butler, especially a proper Butler, to wish to do such a thing... unless." She looked at the toy bear with a dreadful suspicion clouding her brow. "Kitty? What have you been up to now?"

"Don't look at me!" the bear responded tartly, momentarily ceasing her glee. "I happened to mention that those spiders were back. I did not think to mention that fire was not the particular solution you cared for."

"Spiders? What spiders?" Victoria shrieked.

Kitty laughed immoderately. "Such a high-pitched voice you have! The original spiders are still up in the attic, quite possibly dead of old age. But I told you that spiders lay eggs in the thousands. Well, here is the proof."

Victoria clasped her hands in despair. She wrung them together most piteously. "Oh, Oh," she cried.

The bear charged on without remorse. "These current spiders must be the newly-hatched offspring. Or, perhaps not. They were quite large and even more vicious than the others. As to Hoggbend's response...well, that was natural. Victoria, you must agree. I saw your face when you considered just allowing our spiders to suffocate in that box. Probably your notion of a humane ending!"

The elderly woman made one last stab at saving face. "But, fire!"

The bear was having none of that. "Fire, suffocation, international mail. What on earth is the difference? Hoggbend was already quite familiar with the effects of finding a spider in the mailbox. Knowing there was a further infestation, well, I must say, our Butler acted without hesitation." Kitty chortled with glee. "You should see what he did...!"

Victoria's heart stuck in her throat. She turned without a word and plodded, each step a weighted effort to the front gate. The mailbox, post, and several feet of manicured grass all around were scorched black. Kitty came panting after her, out of breath. "Tee hee!" she chuckled. "I told you so!"

"Yes, Kitty, so you have mentioned. I must remind you once again that saying, 'I told you so' is not a valid step along the path to a satisfactory life." The elderly woman shook her old grey head. There was nothing she could think to do about the situation. Absent-mindedly she turned her back on the scene of destruction to face her house. She lifted her eyes and stood appalled. Red, bloodlike drops ran down from the amateurishly painted address numbers and spattered a good deal of the surrounding wall. "It looks like a crime scene!" she exclaimed in wonderment. "You could almost swear that's congealed blood!"

All at once, the elderly woman was overcome with hysteria. She laughed and laughed till tears ran down her face. Miss Kitty, who had been chewing thoughtfully on a stem of charred grass, (just delicious!) stared. Soundlessly, a dripping Hoggbend materialized at her side.

"Modome," he murmured, "the phone."

His head was bent low over that instrument, which he cradled atop one of the small blue velvet pillows usually adorning the couch in the living room. His sleekly combed-back hair was plastered over his bald spot. She squealed without restraint. "OOOH! Who on this planet could want to talk to me!" The Butler continued gravely holding the phone towards her at arms-length, until she recovered enough to take it from him. "Hello? Hello?"

"Mother!" screamed her daughter, "What in the world is going on?"

Without a moment's hesitation, Victoria bellowed, "It's a crime scene! You should see it! And I have no idea how I am now to get the mail!"

Cooked Grass

Taking care not to set anything else aflame, roast a generous mound of long-stemmed grasses in a hot fire till crunchy and well charred. If spiced with a quantity of juicy bugs, so much the better, for they are most nutritious as well as delicious. Ants and aphids are sweetish, while worms are quite salty.

Chapter 22
Infinite Cups of Tea

Days passed. At least, so it appeared to the old woman. There were many, many teas served with impeccable precision and the highest degree of refinement. Delicious baked goods, perfect cups of tea, starched white lace table cloths, polished silver, all sped by, one on top of the other till Victoria felt as if she had stumbled into in an alternate universe; "Tea-Ville". "I don't remember going to bed. Or getting up. Or eating a regular meal. All I seem to be doing lately is attending exquisite tea parties with Kitty, while Hoggbend the Butler waits on us. How odd."

She bit into a shatteringly crisp pastry. Sweet blood-red fruit filling oozed out the sides and dripped down her fingers. She licked them. The sweetness of strawberries was balanced by the salty sharpness of a paper-thin sliver of cheese. A sip of hot sweet creamy tea washed it all down. A sigh of the deepest contentment escaped her pursed lips.

"Kitty, my dear, have you ever tasted such delicious...Kitty? Where are you?" Gazing about the kitchen table, the elderly human realized the tea party seemed to have been arranged for a party of one; one tea cup and saucer, one snowy napkin, one plate of pastries. "Now where can she be?" A sound drew her attention to the floor. "Are you having your tea under the table, my dear?" she queried absently, with only the remotest hint of curiosity. Kitty's plethora of eccentricities having risen to the point of the commonplace, she merely made sure to secure her own plate of pastries with one protective hand before taking a look.

Instead of her eyes encountering the expected sight of the tiny toy bear indulging in a solo and therefore gluttonous tea, she espied Hoggbend the Butler, at a distance, sitting cross-legged on the floor in the sunlight streaming through the open kitchen door. The elderly woman gasped in surprise, then peered closer. "I thought...Oh yes, there you are Hoggbend. I was looking for Kitty." The eccentricities of the Butler were not so well established as to escape without her making a remark. "What is it you are you doing?"

He turned to face her. There was a very red, jagged scar running from his right eye to the corner of his mouth. Victoria pulled back in revulsion.

The Butler coughed discreetly into a large handkerchief. "I am fashioning a wig, Modome, for myself, out of this skein of grey yarn. I took the liberty of removing it from your work basket."

"Oh, I see," Victoria said, though she didn't. After a moment, even though it was such poor form to display ignorance, she asked, "Why, again?"

Patiently, the Butler left off his engrossing work and twisted towards her once more. He coughed again. "A grey wig, it seems, is more befitting a Butler of my stature. If I may; Miss Kitty has become quite severe about my appearance. I'm afraid she was a bit disappointed over my reluctance to try to achieve her embodiment of an ideal Butler. My failure excited her baser instincts." He coughed softly into the hanky, then leaned confidentially towards the old woman. "She does have very sharp teeth, as you have cause to know, Modome, and a short temper. There was a good deal of unpleasantness before I became sufficiently...cowed."

Victoria nodded thoughtfully, perfectly understanding the situation. "I believe the word you are searching for is 'tamed'."

He looked startled. "Yes," he nodded solemnly, "Yes, I believe that is correct."

"It has long been one of that bear's keenest pleasures to tame a wild ferocious Butler, as she did Lily so many years ago." She hesitated. "I hope you will not mind, but I have noticed your scar. Something new. Not an actual scar, I imagine?"

Hoggbend stroked the ghastly thing gingerly. "No, thank you, for your concern. Things with Miss Kitty have not yet gotten that far out of hand! My years of training in the field of beautification have supplied me with most of the tools and skills necessary to fulfill any requirements in the line of makeup artistry. Indeed, one might almost venture to conjecture that the time spent in my youth as a hairdresser might now be seen as an apprenticeship of sorts, in preparation for this, my greatest role. My vocation, if you will." Arrived at that happy conclusion, he returned to his task. His self-satisfied tuneless whistling was interrupted by another cough.

Victoria left off sipping her excellent tea. "Not getting sick, are you, Hoggbend? Catching a cold? Please do take some of this tea with a little honey and lemon."

"Modome is all gracious condescension. Thank you, but no. I am not ill, but am still suffering the aftereffects of that incident with the fire. Fires. Smoke inhalation."

Thunderstruck, Victoria now recalled the last time she had seen the Butler: soaking wet, wreathed in black smoke from the fires Kitty claimed he had set to the mailbox and the backyard shed. She tried her best to conceal the fact that she was suffering an astounding absence of memory from that time until now. "I...I do hope you will make a complete recovery."

The Butler bowed as well as he was able, sitting down and twisted to the side.

Victoria knew she must make a comment, however little she relished the task. After all, the Butler was in her employ and the fires had been set by him. "I hope I am not...well...do I presume too much in asking how it was that you came to the astonishingly irresponsible decision to burn down the mailbox and the shed?" Clearly, Victoria was out of her depth here. The human was glad indeed that Miss Kitty was not present, for she was certain of being called to task. This most definitely was not the way for a person in her position to question an employee. Stiffening her spine, she thus amended, "I mean, why on earth would you do such a thing?"

The Butler left off his task with a show of great reluctance, sighing hugely and dragging himself erect as if from a bog. He stood, heels together, bowing deeply, remaining bent over at the waist with just the top of his shiny bald head showing. "Modome. I had allowed myself to hope that this issue was closed to your satisfaction."

All at once Victoria was irritated beyond measure. "Oh please! Do stand upright Hoggbend! I can't have you all bent over that way! How is one to have a rational conversation?" She waited until he had reared up facing her, pink-cheeked, with errant strands of thinning black hair wafting around his forehead. "That's better. Much better. Now. I have no recollection of that issue being addressed to anyone's satisfaction. I think that I would remember if you had explained why you felt it necessary to set fire to my house. I am not that senile, you know!"

"Indeed." The Butler seemed almost vibrating with the urgent impulse to bow. He permitted himself the liberty of placing his hands on the back of a chair in order to force himself to stay in an upright position. "My assurance of your satisfaction came from Miss Kitty, Modome. If I am mistaken in that assurance, and in your satisfaction with my efforts as your Butler, I shall never live it down and must tender my resignation at once."

"Oh dear!" said Victoria.

"Are we having tea?" chirped a bright voice from the kitchen table. Stricken, the Butler and his mistress turned their eyes to an energetic bear climbing onto the table top. With a gleam of greed in her eyes, she hustled over to Victoria's brimming plate and took a huge bite out of her unfinished pastry. "Mmm!" she said, "My favorite. Blackberry. Hoggbend, you have quite outdone yourself!" At the continued strained silence, she turned her head, purple juices staining her muzzle, and directed questioning eyes at the old woman. "Victoria, whatever is the matter? Were you attempting to keep this for yourself? How secretive you have become with the goodies! And greedy! And, Hoggbend, may I ask why was not I summoned for tea?"

"Oh dear," said Victoria.

Kitty waited, chewing energetically, looking back and forth between the two silent humans, and then she lost interest. She ran her blunted claws over the China plate, idly scraping the surface to gather smears of syrup, producing an ear-piercing squeal. "Humans are so boring and ineffectual," she thought, "Why can't they just be more like bears? Dumdeedum

dumdeedum. Ew! The stinky cheese!" She bustled closer for a sniff, and then a nibble, and then a great big bite, and then most of her head disappeared inside the large wedge of cheese. "Yummy, yummy!" she murmured.

Unable to restrain the impulse any longer, the Butler abruptly bent in half, withdrew to the doorway once more and seated himself in the hot sunlight. He assessed the lump of grey yarn with displeasure before shaking it out and once more picking up his sewing needle.

Victoria sipped her cool tea. Whatever was a woman to do? 　Kitty had burrowed a hole quite through the wedge of cheese to the other side where she lolled, sated, Victoria thought, until she realized the bear was stuck, wedged in the wedge, unable to go forward or back out. It seemed she found it a pleasant sensation for the bear was snoring softly. Hoggbend, so engrossed in his task, failed to notice the elderly woman rising from her chair and drifting off into her living room.

"What a relief to be away from all the drama," she remarked absently. She sank down on the couch next to Barton Cottage.

"Ahem! Modome, if I may?" Startled, the elderly woman found Hoggbend standing, or rather bent over, beside her with a full tray of tea things.

"Oh, of course, Hoggbend, please, do put that down right here." Airily, she indicated the coffee table as she sat up.

However long had she been lying down? And how embarrassing to be caught napping! "Smells lovely. What am I to expect?"

"Modome is all graciousness. I am pleased to present you with hot buttered toasted currant scones with clotted cream and lemon curd, (all of my own making,) India tea with cream and clover honey, crisp strips of peppered bacon, and the cheddar Modome liked so much."

Victoria sniffed appreciatively. "You are quite the eighth wonder, Hoggbend." Because she knew it would make him happy, she added, "Your mother would be proud."

He tilted his head up to thank her, but as the truly horrific scar almost bisecting his face came into view, the woman sharply sucked in her breath. It was then she really, honestly took a good look at the man. For how long had she been overlooking the transformation of her Butler? He was an astonishing creature, apparently all "of his own making" indeed. The masterfully constructed grey wool wig skewed a little to one side.

Noticing her intense scrutiny, he asked, "Is Modome quite well?"

Victoria stuttered, "That...wig...it is truly amazing, Hoggbend. Wonderful." She bit deeply into her thickly buttered scone. "Just amazingly natural."

The Butler smiled ingratiatingly. "Modome is all kindness." He began to back away, still bowed over and clutching the empty tea tray in his hands; thought better of it and returned soundlessly to her side. "Hrump."

"Good gracious! You startled me! I thought you'd gone!"

"If I may be so bold, Modome. The cheddar, as you see, is in two pieces. It had been sliced from a wheel in a wedge, and as an intact wedge, so it had been placed on a tray where it should have been safe, but; as happens so frequently when a certain small bear of large appetite is in the vicinity, Miss Kitty found it and attacked it and ate her way through it and I thought it best to cut it in two after trimming away the gnawed places. Also, Modome's daughter will soon be arriving from the airport."

The Butler's entertaining delivery style left her quite off guard. "What?" Victoria shot to her feet, bumping the coffee table in the process, and slopping tea all over the carpet.

Hoggbend remained frozen in place, bent over the empty tray with his wig askew, but answered imperturbably, "The cheddar, Modome. It is in two pieces because..."

Victoria fairly screamed at him, "Not that! The cheddar...I can see for myself, oh, hang it! What was that about Lily?"

The Butler seemed nonplussed. "She should be here soon..." he drawled cautiously, listening, "Yes, I believe... that may be she I hear just now. If Modome will excuse me..."

There was good reason now for the Butler to regret his ludicrous doubled-up posture, for it prevented him from springing into action and winning the race to open the front door. Victoria, the legitimate owner of the house and the Butler's employer, also lost the race, for Kitty, having nimbly slid down the banister from the upstairs hallway where she had been spying out the front window, was launched with a thud against the door just as Lily opened it with her key.

Gingerbread

Nasty, sharp stuff, like a swig of medicine...except if it's cut in the shape of gingerbread men! And then! What a delight! Especially eating the heads.

Chapter 23

The Original Butler Returns

"The baby and Jim are still at the hotel, Mother. I thought it best to come on ahead and see that everything is…safe." The former Butler trailed off in distraction. Hoggbend came struggling through into the living room with his heavily laden tray straining his arms. The grey wig, freshly powdered and tightly curled into opposing hairy sausages, just brushed the very tips of his fabulously waxed mustache. A jagged crimson scar ran across his face. He bowed deeply as he deposited the tray with a grunt on the coffee table.

"Tea is served." he announced, beaming. The three females gathered there, signaled with nods of their respective heads that all was satisfactory, thus releasing him from his duties. The Butler seemed momentarily disappointed. He frowned, glancing covertly at their faces, but quickly re-masked into the perfectly stolid indifference of the perfect servant, then withdrew when nothing more was forthcoming. The three females waited till the top of his bewigged head, the last of him within view, had disappeared around the corner. Lily rose quietly, tiptoed across and scanned the dim hallway.

"He's gone!" she hissed. "The kitchen door is shut."

Miss Kitty bounced up and down. "Well!" she fairly shouted, "Well now! Let's see what fabulous treats Hoggbend has provided for us!"

"You are so greedy, Kitty!" admonished Victoria. "Oh look! Look at that! The cherry tarts with cream. You have to try these, Lily. I think they are quite his best."

Victoria's daughter stared open-mouthed in disbelief. "Mother! And you too, Kitty! What on earth! Will you please forget the cherry tarts?"

"No, really, Lily," the bear responded, swiftly skipping across the tabletop in her old friend's direction, "you will be...well, I can always eat your share if you aren't hungry." She prepared to swipe the delectable pastry dripping sweet red juices into the slick of white cream off Lily's plate.

Only by a deft maneuver was the well-practiced former Butler able to prevent her tiny plastic childhood toy from completing her act of thievery. Then she stared. On a silver tray covered with a paper doily, were artfully arranged store-bought cookies of the cheapest kind, a variety of generic packaged ones, improbably neon-colored, and dolloped with blobs of canned whipped cream and splotches of jelly. Alongside these delights were crumbly, stale-looking crackers topped with wormy sausages of a spray-on cheese-product and artificial bacon bits. A square slab of semi-plastic cheese oozed beads of oil.

Her mother chewed lustily; her eyes closed with contentment. What on earth had happened to her mother? The once sensibly-coiffed, plain and demure gardening enthusiast had disappeared. The old woman before her sported a fantastically curled and teased hairstyle rising high from her brow in astonishing sweeping wings! Two pink spots highlighted her cheeks, a purple lump loomed on her forehead, a swath of scarlet hid her lips, and her eyelids were painted sky-blue. Concealing her distress, the young woman took a deep breath. "Listen to me. Please. Both of you. This is serious."

Two pairs of eyes rose as one to focus on the earnest former Butler. The human's eyes were drawn irresistibly back down to the table, where that cunning bear had already bitten into the largest pastry by far. The toy's beady plastic eyes glinted. One might almost, having been mesmerized by the constancy of the stare, miss the quick movements of paws gathering together all that was within reach.

"There's not much time," Lily pleaded, "We have to discuss what we are to do."

"It seems a hopeless case, then, so let's eat!" Kitty bawled, as she stuffed fruit tarts and ham and cheese dainties into her gaping maw with alarming rapidity. To no one's surprise she was soon choking, coughing, and spraying crumbs, and since her chosen seat was actually upon the silver tray, all the crumbs settled onto all the delicate pastries and on the surface of the poured tea in the fine porcelain cups.

Instead of the expected roar of maternal outrage, Lily was astonished to see her mother throw back her head and roar with laughter! The turreted pile of grey hair swayed dangerously, flopping to one side and dangling over one eye. It was just another in the string of vulgarities that were to follow. Victoria pushed her bouffant hairdo back into place and she and Kitty chuckled cozily as they swept the regurgitated crumbs under a napkin and proceeded on with their interrupted feast as if nothing had happened. The demands of the former Butler were quite forgot.

Sharply sucking in a deep breath, Lily turned on her heel and strode down the hall to the kitchen door. "I see I must take matters into my own hands," she murmured, "For some reason Mother has gone off the deep end, and Kitty... well, Kitty is as bad as ever." Cautiously, she pushed the door open. Whatever it was she had been expecting to find there was not at all what she found, for the kitchen was empty. It was an astonishing set-back. She blinked her eyes, then rubbed them furiously in disbelief.

"Where on earth...?" Clearly, the second Butler invited to occupy that exalted position in the confounding history of her family was not busily conducting his official business, as had been expected, nor had he been doing so for some time for the kitchen was as pristine as an advertisement for unused kitchens in a glossy magazine. Lily stepped through the glass doors out to the patio and on into the walled garden, remaining deep in thought. There came a second shock! The garden was a mess! The young woman was horrified by the level of disorder in her mother's ordinarily immaculate outdoor space. Her eyes were drawn irresistibly to a blackened area heaped with debris where the garden shed used to be. She examined it. A fire. "Oh! Mother mentioned something about fires." The conclusion was obvious. "Kitty!" she roared.

"Ahem!"

The soft sound coming from right behind caused her to jerk upright in alarm. Hoggbend, for it was none other than that elusive, mysterious Butler, was deeply bent over at the waist. He coughed discreetly into a large white handkerchief. "The sandwiches have been cut, and are now served," he announced in the direction of her shoes, "if Modome will please to return to the living room?"

Unceremoniously, the former Butler reached out and grasped the lapels of the present Butler. Without mercy, she pulled him upright, and violently shook him! "Ernie! What is going on here?" With a sort of gurgle, Ernie Hoggbend, Butler, rolled his eyes back in his head, slipped from her fingers in a cold dead faint, and landed at her feet.

A shriek of horror issued from the doorway. Victoria stood there frozen. Kitty, ever less delicate, as in keeping true to her animal instincts, raced forth with rage trembling every line of her four inch frame. "Lily!" she shrieked. "Account for this at once! Why have you killed our Butler?"

Pizza

Something to hold pepperoni, but delicious in its own right. One cannot have too much cheese on a pizza, or pepperoni, and the crust must be perfection itself. Oh, who am I kidding? Pizza is a thing to convey pepperoni to one's mouth.

Chapter 24
Original, Or New and Improved?

It was a forlorn quartet who assembled in the basement later that day. In an act of desperate, unmannered defiance, Hoggbend had torn off his magnificently powdered and curled wig, followed by his mustache, as well as having scraped away at the painted-on jagged scar. Only the keenest challenge to his conscience on Kitty's part had compelled him to stay initially, and only the physical impossibility of strong-arming a revered old woman prevented him from bolting numerous times during the next few hours-long inquisition. Lily was merciless.

"You have been living here all along? In Mom's basement?"

"My duties require constant attendance, as you well know. I came to the conclusion early on that it was quite beyond my capabilities to move instantaneously back and forth between my residence and this home, magically flying through the air (as you seem to be suggesting), in order to be in two places at once to provide your mother with the quality and quantity of service she deserves, at any hour of the day and night. When you were Butler, were you not in residence?"

"That is beside the point, I..."

Miss Kitty had returned to Lily's feet from her tour of the secret facilities. "The Butler's lair!" she pronounced. By hoisting herself up the young woman's pants and over her knees and shirt front, she was able to reach her jacket pocket where she snuggled comfortably and thus attain speaking height level with the trio of gargantuan humans. "If I may, Lily?" she shouted. "This matter is one easily taken care of. I can see it all clearly now. So clearly…"

"And you!" the young woman blustered, clearly itching to pluck the bear from out of her pocket, "I will be having a word with you later. Privately!" She gulped air, calming herself. "But right now I must hear it all from Ernie. From Hoggbend. I need to know…" Once again, the never-winnable battle for self-control was lost; she grasped her old friend by the neck of her dress and removed her to a tabletop. "I can assure you, however Miss Kitty, that I am certain that he cannot account for any of this without your connivance. It is not possible."

Once more Victoria was in the position of having almost accidentally learned the hard way that she had underestimated that small toy bear. "Is it true, old friend?" she bleated plaintively. "Have you once again been the instrument of bringing yet more dangerous creatures from the outside into the belly of my home? Without my knowledge?"

Kitty had the decency to blush and hang her head, a pretty picture of contrition, until the onlookers realized she was surreptitiously chewing on something concealed inside the lace-covered bodice of her gingham dress. "Oh Victoria," she crunched around a mouthful, "Outside, inside, indoors, outdoors...what's the difference? Humans are so hung up on trivialities."

Outraged human voices drowned each other out. Victoria won through sheer force of lung power, roaring from atop the moral high ground. "Miss Katherine A. Bear! Lily! Hoggbend! All of you! I will not stand for it! Not a moment longer! Not under my own roof!"

For once the guilty parties seemed shaken by the real anger in the venerable woman's tone. They stared at her open-mouthed. Not even the ridiculously styled and now disarranged mass of her hair bobbing and straggling down her cheeks could lessen the gravity of her anger. Before Lily or Kitty could utter a word, Hoggbend rushed in, surprisingly, to their defense.

"I must take the lion's share of the recriminations, Modome, I really must. Though Lily did indeed present me with the opportunity, an invitation that was kindness itself, and Miss Kitty certainly paved the way for me to enlarge upon it when she invited me in and made a vast many interesting suggestions, it was I myself who took it to the next level, by intruding so completely and secretly into this domicile. I must assure you that there were no evil intentions. You must believe me for I am devastated if you do not. Dear Modome, surely you cannot think me capable of any treachery whatsoever towards you! I wanted only to be of service, and in order to do that, I determined that quietly moving in here was the best solution for all concerned."

No one spoke. Thus encouraged by their silence, he continued. "And then, you know, there was the undeniable fact that after so neglecting my outside duties, and in effect, abandoning, my job at the post office without giving notice, there was no more job, no more paychecks, no more money to pay the bills, and so I lost my apartment, and then the car, and things snowballed until you find me here, in your basement, attempting to be useful as well as inconspicuous." He hesitated, glancing from stony wooden expression to quizzically wooden expression to molded absentminded plastic expression. "It is a desire I have struggled to achieve. I hope, to everyone's satisfaction."

There were embarrassed murmurs of agreement, and even a stifled, 'Hurrah!' from Miss Kitty. The Butler was not off the hook yet.

"How could you...I mean, how could you..." Lily stopped to collect her thoughts, which were somewhat disorganized. "Ernie. How is it possible that my simple request for you to look in on my mother now and then when going about on your daily rounds, has resulted in you living in her basement, acting as her butler?" Puzzled faces all around revealed an honest lack of understanding. "And apparently, as her hairdresser? And beautician?"

"You thought I needed looking in on, and by a stranger?" was Victoria's reaction. "What am I? A child?"

"Why should Victoria need anyone looking in on her? Have you forgotten that I am here, Lily? I have been taking care of her, admirably, for all these many years now," was Kitty's indignant response.

"What?" shouted the old woman. "Taking care of me?"

"Mother...I only wanted...just an extra set of eyes and ears...nothing personal...I know you are quite capable. Kitty...anyway..." She drifted to a stop. "Anyway, I certainly never intended for...Ernie! How did this happen?"

The former postal employee had quite forgot himself and was slunk down in abject misery upon a footstool. "It happened," he explained patiently, 'because I answered the call when you asked me to."

"That is not...!" Lily shook the cobwebs from her head. "That is not...that did not happen! You know that is not..." The battle was joined.

Of the interested parties, Victoria and Kitty seemed the least concerned in the outcome. Kitty had ferreted out a rack of still-juicy fruits Hoggbend had been drying in the sun: apples and pears, apricots and plums, and arranged them on a platter with a bowl of powdered sugar for dipping. She and her human friend dipped and munched, dipped and munched, while raptly studying the two warriors.

"This is quite as good as any moving picture, Victoria dear. I must say I cannot decide who will prevail, or to whom I shall give the honors."

"Well, I must choose Lily, as you very well know, she has had the longer acquaintance with me. With both of us in fact, and I would have thought she should have had a claim on your loyalty as well, since you and she have that unbreakable bond. Since childhood." Here Kitty casually dropped her paw from the plate of fruit to rest it atop the woman's forearm, a tactic with which Victoria was well familiar. The pink-skinned human hastened to qualify her opinion. "However, in all fairness, I must acknowledge that Hoggbend is, most likely, your creation, is he not? And so I quite understand where your loyalties must lie." She gently disengaged her arm from the claws of her friend, brushing away the dusting of powdery sugar.

The shouting had ground to a halt. Victoria and Kitty raised inquisitive eyes to their former and present butlers. That pair were visibly red-faced and angry.

Hoggbend's Dainties

Miss Kitty has requested my recipe for the dainties I have been honored to serve her and my mistress, Victoria. Unfortunately I have misplaced my recipes and so must decline.

Chapter 25

Born to Buttle

"If Modome would care to speak first?" Hoggbend inquired stiffly of the young woman.

"It's Lily, to you, Ernie! Lily! Oh, do allow me, please, Hoggbend!" Lily bit her tongue, struggling for mastery "But; perhaps, yes, now that I think about it. It's only fair. Yes, it should come from you."

The Butler rose to his feet. Even minus the powdered wig and scar, he was an imposing figure. "As you wish. Modome…Lily." He bowed coldly to Lily. "Dearest Modome." he bowed deeper and held it much longer for Victoria. Inclining his head slightly, he muttered, "Miss Kitty!" in a curious tone, vibrating with unspoken meaning. "Shall we then revisit how first I made my acquaintance with you?"

The nods of assent were universal, as was the burning curiosity to hear the story in its entirety.

"All these many years past, I, Ernie Hoggbend, a sad and lonely, misunderstood boy…"

"Perhaps not that far back, if you please," Lily interrupted.

Kitty and Victoria jumped in to intervene: "Please! Do continue. We want to hear it all!" were their combined exclamations.

Imperturbably, the Butler obliged. "...a sad and lonely boy, without friends or playmates, was invited by a small girl to attend a tea party at her home given by her friend, Miss Kitty. I knew not what to expect, but as a diversion from troubled thoughts and the constant bullying by the neighborhood boys, I accepted. Thus began a series of remarkable experiences. Through Modome...Lily's eyes, for it was she who took pity on me, I discovered an entire world of enchantment, of civility, of imagination; and all over an imaginary pot of tea. The sensation was delightful, I can assure you! Though the tea parties were few and far between, I attended them constantly, in my mind. I practiced the mannerisms and the manners, which predictably resulted in a marked increase in the day-to-day harassment visited upon me by the local thugs; I devoured the works of Jane Austen, I dressed appropriately to the period, I relished my self-appointed role as Mister Darcy or Captain Wentworth, or... Yes, you ladies may scoff at my aspirations, but I can assure you, they were entirely worthy of merit. And so I achieved adulthood, almost as an afterthought to my chosen role in life as an Austen hero. And I was a failure.

Men, you know, must be good at something, other than courtly manners and polished diction. When you rang me up, Lily, it was such a blessing! A bolt out of the blue on the wings of angels! The role I had been burdened with, of delivering mail, was a daily trial. I seized upon the notion of being useful to the woman who had nurtured you and your extraordinary childhood imagination, with the determination of a bulldog. And then, providentially, you, Miss Kitty, you flung open the door, and I seized upon the implicit role of Butler with a relief approaching madness."

The three listeners reacted in their respective ways: Lily squirmed in embarrassment, Victoria sighed with rapture, and Kitty stopped chewing.

"I never imagined...well, how could I?" Lily began.

Her mother shushed her. "You felt you were born to be a butler? My Butler? In particular?"

Hoggbend beamed. "Exactly, Modome. If I may say so, since the idea of: Miss Kitty, and the warrior women, and all the small plastic friends, are a possibility, why not me? I am no more or less fantastical than they are. If I may be so bold."

Victoria murmured, "Of course! That is flawless logic."

"But, my devotion to you, dear Modome, has also been the cause of my undoing in the larger world outside of this house, for with the loss of my job, car, apartment, all the trappings of modern existence, I fear I had no other choice but to establish myself here, within the shelter of your home and bosom so that I could fulfill my function. You see, I feel I have been led to be your Butler by a conspiracy of all the fates on earth."

The silence greeting this astonishing revelation was deafening. Hoggbend had lowered his head theatrically during the finale of his recitation, but was driven by curiosity to raise his eyes, peering closely at his audience to gauge their reaction. Victoria looked enchanted, Lily was scarlet with some nameless emotion, and Miss Kitty...Miss Kitty was absent.

Mouse Stew

Take one dead mouse. Put it in the stew pot when Victoria is not looking. Cover your ears and run for your life! (Mouse stew sounds better than it tastes.)

Chapter 26

Fire, For the Last time

What followed was, at best, unseemly. While Lily jumped to her own and her mother's defense in the face of such outlandish claims against them: harmless women who, all unwitting, had become the victims of a scheming opportunist. Fates and a benevolent universal conspiracy need not be invoked. Hoggbend allowed himself to shed a tear or two, all the while protesting his innocence and the inevitability of his position. Victoria rapidly ate everything within her immediate reach, stuffing her maw with dried fruits, large chunks of cheese, crackers, and washing it all down with swigs of cold tea slurped directly from the spout of the tea pot.

A thundering of rapidly approaching plastic horse's hooves finally brought the group to attention. The Bideable horse, looking both proud and abashed at the same time, galloped up to the table leg and slid to a stop. His rider descended in a martial swirl of skirts, with eyes flashing.

When all were silenced to her liking, Miss Kitty stomped imperiously back and forth between them. "While you humans were engaged in your insignificant bickering over the past, I have been attending to the present, and therefore much more relevant issue. Victoria dear, you will make yourself sick!" The tiny bear hoisted herself up to the tabletop to stare in disbelief at the empty plates. She lapped at the drops still trickling down the spout of the teapot, then shook her head in disgust.

"There are larger issues to hand, Lily, than this unwarranted attack upon a perfectly wonderful Butler. I see that I, again, must be the bearer of bad news. We have been besieged by none other than those dratted spiders!"

Hoggbend shot to his feet. "Are you c-c-certain?" he stammered.

"Of course! I did warn you."

The Butler sketched a bow. He faced Victoria and Lily, meeting their eyes with a desperately appealing gaze. "Modome, I fear there is no time to lose!" He gulped. "Miss Kitty did indeed warn me of this event. I must...we all must move quickly, or all shall be lost indeed."

His urgency was irresistible. He crammed his grey wig upon his head and dashed up the cellar stairs, the two women trailing behind him. Miss Kitty paused for a moment, seizing the opportunity, to load the front of her dress with crumbs of cheese and a few nuts before springing onto the horse's back and galloping after them.

The humans raced to the front of the house but were stymied when the Butler was unable to budge the rigid knob of the front door. "Too late!" he cried. "We must exit by the kitchen door!" As they ran the intrepid Hoggbend shouted, "But I fear that we are already too late!"

Victoria and her daughter were dry-mouthed with anxiety. What unimaginable horror awaited them on the other side of the front door? The old woman thought she might faint, sagging against her daughter's supporting arm, but was strengthened by an overwhelming curiosity.

"This is how Kitty must feel all the time!" she gasped to Lily, being somewhat out of breath. "No wonder she's so cranky all the time. Fear! Curiosity! Excitement! All mixed together." By this time the kitchen door was opened, and the party fairly flew around through the garden, panting to the front of the house. Miss Kitty was already there atop her rearing steed.

The bear cackled with smug and angry glee. "I told you so, Hoggbend! I told you so!"

That bedraggled Butler nodded sadly in agreement. "You did indeed."

The front of the house, from the ground to the rafters, was draped in a thick, billowing, grey veil of spider webs. An impenetrable mass, the webs were adorned with the desiccated corpses of countless insects, legs especially, as well as antennae and shiny iridescent carapaces. Lily and her mother clung together in appalled silence.

Kitty shouted, "Hoggbend, take courage! you know what it is you must do!"

"I am already on it!" he shouted in return. He approached the thickly draped curtain brandishing a lighter in his hand.

"Forgive me!" he bellowed to no one in particular and lighting a dry faggot of straws tied together in a kind of club, swept it grandly through the webs. With a thunderous 'swoosh', the thick veils caught, erupting skyward in tongues of brilliant red and yellow flame, and then almost instantaneously, falling, falling, dissolving, into a black heap of ashes on the ground.

Jam Making

Go to the store and buy a jar. Trust me, no one can make jam without first making a colossal mess of the stove; floor; walls; most of the kitchen utensils; one's best morning tea-frock; and one's relationship with a grouchy old human. So save yourself the bother and just buy a jar. Peach is best.

Chapter 27

Miss Kitty Meets the Baby

The front of the house was of course pretty much destroyed. Those original spiders, the unwitting architects of all that was to befall them including their own doom, had multiplied with a vengeance and sent forth their vast multitudes of offspring upon such voluminous draglines and substantial webbing until it seemed the very rafters must bow under the weight. The application of fire, while effectively annihilating everything spider-related, also singed the wood, blistered the paint, curled the shingles, and blackened the stonework. Amazingly, the only things left quite untouched were the scarlet-painted foot-high numbers still bloodily dripping Victoria's address across the fire-damaged front.

Kitty was immensely proud of that. "Oh. See! There you are, Hoggbend! You wanted the house number to be made plainly visible and now you have it!"

Lily for once was speechless. Victoria was chuckling weakly, sweeping her watery eyes over the astounding sight before her. Hoggbend hung his head, clutching the grey wig between soot-stained fingers.

Miss Kitty marched out to the street and looked piercingly up and down it. "I must say, where are the fire trucks? Victoria, my dear, you know you have been threatening me forever with fire trucks and police! And yet there are no signs of them. When I happened to set fire to a few blades of grass, in the garden, in the back of the house, behind the wall, you were quite sarcastic, yet here the whole front of the house has burned up and no sirens. None at all."

The old woman joined her at the curb, right beside the place where her mailbox used to be, and followed her friend's example, looking all about for some sign that more than the four of them were aware of events. "Well. Just so. We could be living on an island for all the notice we are paid. Kitty, my dear, I believe we could with impunity run around in our bare skins!"

"Yes, my dear, as I do."

"As you do what?"

"Run around in my bear skin."

"Oh, ha ha ha, Lily, did you hear? Kitty said..."

But Lily was not listening. The former Butler stared open-mouthed at the blackened front of her childhood home. In a moment she was restored to her senses. The accurate aim and throwing ability of her former toy was undiminished. She rubbed the sore spot on her brow where the stone had made contact. "Don't worry, Kitty. You may put your mind at rest. You shall have all the attention you deserve and desire, for I believe they shall soon be after us with butterfly nets. All of us."

That disheartened creature, Hoggbend, was using his wig as a dust-rag, swiping at the sooty strings of cobweb still dangling down from the rafters, and polishing the brass door fittings. The stricken look of sadness contorting his face struck Lily as so outlandishly comical, it brought her to her knees choking with sobs of laughter.

She sat on the grass. At the curb stood her mother, who she now noticed had grown amazingly stout during her absence. The ancient woman was holding an animated conversation with a toy bear sitting atop her shoulder clutching her ear.

"How? However...have things gotten to this point?" the young woman muttered to herself. "At least I can be grateful that Jim and the baby are not here..." Just then a taxi pulled up and Jim and the baby emerged from it.

Ecstatically, Victoria cradled her squirming grandchild in her arms while Jim approached his wife with a cautious half-smile of disbelief.

"Don't ask!" warned Lily, rising to her feet and holding up a preemptory hand. "It is much better not to ask!" Her husband's gaze traveled over the front of the house, resting for a moment on the blood-dripping address numbers, before alighting fixedly on the fantastical figure of Hoggbend, bent at the waist in a prolonged bow so that only the top of his mottled bald head was showing. He thoughtfully put an arm around his wife and turned her, so the pair were facing the old woman who was lovingly kissing and snuggling with their child. The baby was cooing, and babbling, all his attention directed at the sullen lump of a toy bear stuck on his grandmother's shoulder.

Quite suddenly and with startling precision, a chubby infant hand closed upon the toy and raised it to the drooly lips. Miss Kitty had only time for one horrified, pleading glance in the humans' direction before her head disappeared, fiercely gummed in the toothless mouth.

The Secret to Gardening.

Get someone else to do it. It is a hard, thankless, dirty job and it should be avoided if at all possible. Make sure to give broad hints about the appeal of fresh vegetables, and when they have been harvested, smack your lips and eat as much as you can. Butter is the key.

Chapter 28

The End, At Last

Suffice it to say, all would soon be made right with the appearance of the house, which required little more than a thorough scrubbing, a good deal of paint, and just a bit of carpentry. An exterminator was called in to make certain the plague of giant spiders were routed for good, a new mailbox was installed, and a simply magnificent garden shed was built on the site of the old one, though it is now used more as an outdoor sauna and pool-house by the new owners.

Lily and her young family returned to their lives abroad, where the subject is often canvassed, interrupted often as not by self-recriminations and many scalding tears.

And Victoria was placed in a nursing home dedicated to the care of those elderly humans who have lost their short-term memories as well as their minds. Of course, that diagnosis is far from accurate in her case. She is often quite happy, for she has her dear friend Miss Kitty for her constant companion.

Though clinical criteria have indeed imprisoned her body in this place, her mind is as boundless as ever, her thoughts as wide-ranging, as is evident in her over-heard conversations with the bear. Their loudly debated points of disagreement are recorded in Victoria's chart, which often results in a slight increase in the human's medication.

The warrior women, the Bideable horse, and all the assorted small plastic friends who figured so largely in past narratives, have gone off with Lily to a new home abroad, where they are glumly contemplating a future filled with infant indignities, toddler atrocities, and the prospect of the garbage can when finally spent of their usefulness and interest. Electronic devices are even now rapidly replacing them.

That strange figure of a man who is often seen hovering over the old woman and her tiny toy bear, in the nursing home, does what he can to make them as comfortable as possible before hurrying off to his other duties, for Ernie Hoggbend has found his true calling at last!

He reverently ministers to the hair-dressing and makeup needs of all the vain elderly residents of the nursing home. It is with some reluctance that he has given up the theatrical flourishing of the grey wig and the mustache and the jagged scar, but he finds it a small price to pay for the satisfaction of gainful employment.

His assertion to the contrary, that he was fated to play the part of Victoria's Butler, has slipped his mind, for he has never been happier in finding himself genuinely useful and even beloved by a great many people. The hairstyles are a bit on the fantastic side, but an artist must feel free to express himself, and the operators of the nursing home are glad to have him.

In Hoggbend's free hours, when one should expect him to return to his own home for rest and relaxation, he creeps away instead, down a seldom-used hall in a private wing to Victoria's quarters, where he quietly dons "the Butler" role to his and the old woman's satisfaction.

Indeed, he has found a perfectly satisfactory way to continue on there, having secretly appropriated a large closet beside Victoria's reclining chair as his own quarters. From there he fancies that he may continue to be useful and unobtrusive as well as immediately at hand.

It is only Miss Kitty who is dissatisfied with any part of the permanent new arrangement. That bear forcefully remonstrates with Hoggbend that she alone is capable of caring for Victoria. She also tries without ceasing to inform the rest of the world of her grievances, most of which involve the disgustingly bland pureed food she is forced to eat, but except for Victoria and Hoggbend, and the rarely visiting former Butler and her family, no one can hear or understand her.

THE END

Part Two

A voice, barely above a whisper, in the dark. "Is it time, Kitty?"

"Yes, dear one, it is time."

"I'm afraid."

"Buck up, for goodness sake!"

"I'll try. It's hard."

"It can't be any harder than being trapped in a cardboard box with plastic wrapped over your face. Or stuck in a wooden chest with the lid fastened shut for years at a time in a cold dark attic..."

Kitty was prepared to go on and on, covering all the old grievances; but a very deep, and quite final-sounding sigh, a terminal in-drawing of breath, interrupted her harangue. The toy bear waited, listening in vain for an exhale. The human, Victoria, at last, was silent.

There was a doily-covered tray upon which rested a porcelain teapot, cups and saucers and...could it be? Daringly, Miss Kitty picked up a delicate pastry to examine the bottom. "This scone is delicious and is perfectly baked. I've never seen such perfect pastry!" A moment later, "Or tasted such wonderful...umm. Do try this."

"Oh! Kitty! I'm glad! You are here with me! Does that mean that you too...Everything is so beautiful! I feel so very happy!"

"I knew how it would be! And now, dear friend, since we've finished our tea, let us take a walk in this lovely garden." The bear chuckled, a low gurgly little trill. "I haven't mentioned it, though I am sure you must be bursting with delight, at the change in your size!"

Victoria was puzzled. She strolled blithely, without pain or anxiety through the enchanted garden, stopping when she felt like it to sniff a rose or rub pine sap through her hair. "My size? Aren't you aware that it is indeed you, who have altered?"

"Surely not. This garden, the trees, and plants are all..."

The human hastened to smooth over her friend's distress. She smiled gaily. "I believe we agree on this matter, my dear, for we are both of a same size, and in proportion to our surroundings, for once. That, I can assure you, gives me the greatest satisfaction."

Kitty wrapped her paws around her friend in a snug embrace. They walked together, arm in arm, the sun warm on their faces. "I too, am quite content. Now what think you? How about a sort of reunion with all our old friends?"

"What a delightful idea, Kitty! You are always full of the best schemes. However do you think of them?"

The bear cocked her head, considering. "I'm not sure. Perhaps, because of you? Now, what say you to a very special tea party? Oh! Look! The warrior women are here too! Tuk-Thuk has just dropped her spear on her foot!"